Cowboy for a Season

Janalyn Knight

Published by Janalyn Knight, 2019.

To my amazing daughter Merrissa - my surprise baby and best friend.

Chapter One

HANNAH PLACED THE LONG-stemmed white rose atop the lid of the casket. Her pale, freckled face, companion to her copper hair, turned fiery red when she cried, so if there was a blessing today, it was that she couldn't shed any tears.

A hot wind gusted, bringing a cloud of dust with it and flattening her black funeral dress to her petite frame. The pastor's final speech dimmed in her consciousness. A chapter of her life was over. Any sadness she felt paled against the sense of betrayal that her husband's infidelity and cruel words had caused her. His year-long public affair with a woman in town along with his blaming Hannah because they couldn't have children had killed her love for him long before Ty died three days ago.

She had asked Ty many times to repair the starter on their old John Deere tractor, but he had put it off. Standing beside it, he started the thing with a screw driver each time he drove it. The day it killed him, he forgot to shift the tractor into neutral before starting the engine, and the sharp discs on the plow had run over him. Hannah, used to his long absences, hadn't found him until the next day.

As the pastor's words died away, she stumbled through the awkward condolences from neighbors and friends in a daze. How would she cope in this new life of hers? The one thing

Ty did this past year was tractor work while she struggled hard to manage all the other chores on the ranch. Now she'd have to prepare the wheat fields and plant them, too. A crushing weight settled on her shoulders.

The crowd at the gravesite thinned, and Hannah moved toward the cemetery drive, her parents at her side.

Her mom said, "Honey, let's get you home, and I'll fix you something to eat."

Not caring about food, Hannah responded distantly, "Okay, Momma."

Taking her hand, her father said, "We'll stay as long as you need, baby. Don't you worry."

"I'll be fine, Daddy." All her strong emotions had flown with the desert wind whipping around them, leaving her empty and vague. As she stood next to her father's truck, a hand touched her arm. It was Todd Matthews.

"Excuse me, Hannah. I don't mean to hold you up, but I wanted to say I'm so sorry about your loss. I know things will be hard for you without Ty." Handing her a paper, he said, "Here's my number. A friend of mine is staying with me. He rides the Professional Bull Rider's circuit, but he's recovering from some injuries right now. He knows his way around a ranch. He's not up to heavy stuff, but he's fine for most work. I think he'd be a lot of help to you. Anyway, call me if you're interested." With a pat on her back, he turned away.

"Thanks, Todd," she said faintly. Stuffing the paper in her purse, she opened the truck door and sat in the back seat, gazing out the window, without seeing, as her father drove. Life as she knew it was over. But, wasn't that a good thing? Her life had been hell this past year, knowing Ty made love to another woman and turned his back to Hannah in their own bed. Her heart had been shredded when he blamed her because no child blessed their marriage.

People in town must wonder why she hadn't divorced Ty. He hadn't hidden his affair. But, in some sick way, she almost didn't blame him. She hated herself, too, for her infertility. Her body had betrayed her, just as her husband had.

As her father pulled up in front of the faded-gold adobe ranch house, she got out, stiff and unfeeling, wanting nothing more than to go to bed.

Her mother said, "Honey, why don't you go change, and I'll fix us some lunch. I wish you had invited people over after the service. Still, quite a few friends are coming to drop off food this evening."

The last thing Hannah wanted was to see people. Why did her mother think she didn't have a reception? "Mom, I'm not hungry. Do you mind if I lay down for a while?"

Her mother pulled her into a long hug as Hannah came around the truck. "You do that, dear. Take care of yourself any way you need to. I'm so sorry you're going through this."

Thank God Mom understood. Hannah had missed having her mother close these past four years. After the death of her brother, Ben, they gave her the ranch and moved to Wyoming. Nothing had turned out like Hannah's dreams. Her marriage had failed, she couldn't have children, and her only family lived far away.

Once in her bedroom, she stepped out of her funeral dress and left it on the floor. This room wasn't a refuge. It held memories of hateful words, nights spent alone while her husband buried himself in another woman, and reoccurring nightmares of a long, childless life.

As she slid between the cool sheets and lay her head on the pillow, her mind began the torture she endured every time she closed her eyes. Visions of tiny infants and beautiful toddlers filled her head. She touched soft skin, kissed small faces, and cuddled little bodies to her chest. All she'd ever wanted was to be a mother. Many of her school friends had dreams of careers, but not Hannah. Raising babies with a loving husband had been her only dream. A familiar pain dug deep in her heart. That dream was impossible now. What man would want her barren body? What use was her life? What reason did she have to go on living? Without the release of tears, her dulled senses reached for the black void of sleep.

HANNAH OPENED HER EYES in darkness and struggled to make sense of her reality. She glanced at the alarm. It was past eight in the evening. Still, she didn't want to get up. Couldn't face another human being. Yet, something of the old Hannah rose in her, and she threw the covers back and sat on the edge of the bed. She turned on the light and took stock of the room, noting her discarded dress and deciding to leave it where it lay. She drew in a long breath and expelled it. No way was she getting dressed. Or showering. Picking out a sleepshirt, she pulled it over her head and threw on a robe. Her parents were talking in the living room. Closing her eyes, she stood a moment, building her emotional reserves, then headed down the stairs to join them.

Rising from the couch, her mom gave her a hug. "I'll bet you're hungry. Let me fix you a plate. You won't believe all the food we have. So many people stopped by tonight, honey. And don't worry, I wrote down all their names so you can send thank you notes."

Oh my God, thank you notes. Feeling overwhelmed, she sank down in an overstuffed leather chair and plopped her feet on the ottoman. Of course, she would send thank you notes. Everyone had been so kind. She'd just have to find time to do them. "Mom, do you have these people's addresses?"

"Most likely. I'll check," her mother called from the kitchen.

Hannah's brain started to work again. She got up and found a piece of paper and a pen and wrote down *Buy thank you notes.*

Cutie Pie, her mother's little Yorkshire Terrier, came trotting up to Hannah's chair, looking for cuddles. Her mother had always wanted one of the tiny dogs. When her parents moved to Wyoming, she bought one, as if losing her son had freed her to take care of herself. Hannah picked up Cutie Pie and snuggled him under her chin. *Will I do that, too, now? Take care of myself?*

Her father said, "I fed down at the barn, honey. Everything's fine. One of the heifers looks close to calving, so I'll keep an eye on her tomorrow. You just tell me what needs doing around here, and I'll handle it."

"I love you, Daddy. I'll be all right. But I can always use help." That's when she remembered the paper Todd had given her. Should she hire a hand? Her parents couldn't stay forever. The real question was, could she afford to hire someone? Reality on her ranch meant she couldn't run it herself. She already had all she could do. There was no help for it. Someone else would have to prepare her fields and plant her wheat.

Her mom and dad had their own life now. Losing their son on a battlefield in Afghanistan had shattered them, and they had finally found a way to be happy in the new life they'd built in Wyoming. She couldn't pull them away from that, especially back to this house where Ben grew up.

Before she could rethink it, she got up and pulled the note out of her purse then dialed Todd.

He answered, "Hello?

"Hey, this is Hannah. I'd like to meet your friend, if the offer's still open. My parents need to get back to Wyoming, and I have to put my wheat in. I assume he can run a tractor?"

"Yep, he does. Would you like us to stop by in the morning, say around eight thirty?"

She swallowed. This was happening. "That sounds good. And, hey, thanks for thinking of me."

"You bet. See you tomorrow."

After she hung up, fizzles of anxiety hit her stomach. They'd never had a hand on the place. She and Ty were a team—that is until he lost interest and spent the majority of his time in town. Now she had to figure out how to be the boss and, somehow, she didn't think being a boss to a professional bull rider was going to be that easy. Those PBR cowboys were a breed apart. They had to be to climb on two thousand pounds of exploding, living, breathing hell every week. Maybe being injured had toned down this guy's ego a bit.

Her dad asked, "You going to hire someone, honey?"

"I think so. I want you and Mom to go back to Wyoming in a couple of days. Your life is there now, and I need to be able to handle this place on my own. That means hiring help. I should have done it this past year. I never told you all what was going on."

Holding up his hand, her dad called out, "Janie, come on in here. Hannah has something to tell us."

When her mom had settled on the leather couch, Hannah said, "Ty really left me more than a year ago." When her parents looked confused, she told them the whole story of the past year's events. After she finished, she said, "You're wondering why I didn't divorce him, and I don't have a good answer. It's just I've been in a pretty dark place and couldn't see my way out."

Her mom got up and came over to Hannah, hugging her. "Sweetheart, I wish you had told us all this. We would have been here for you. You shouldn't have gone through this alone. Why, we sit around on our little ranch and don't do a thing all year. We could visit you here in Barbwire any time since we don't have livestock in Wyoming. Promise me you won't ever do that again."

Tears stung Hannah's eyes, and she nodded. She should have told her parents. Looking back, she didn't know why she hadn't, except that she was so hurt and, at the same time, so numb. She'd gone through the motions each day in survival mode.

Brushing Hannah's hair back from her face her mom said, "Sweetheart, it's been years since you've really smiled. I want you to be happy again, and I know you can do that. Your whole life is ahead of you. You remember to say your prayers. Anything is possible in this life of ours, honey." She kissed her daughter's forehead and stepped back. "Come on in the kitchen. Your plate's ready, and I want you to eat. No *buts*."

THE NEXT MORNING DAWNED hot and dusty, the usual on Hannah's desert ranch. She and her father had fed the stock and were loading a round bale on the hay truck when Todd drove down the drive in a cloud of dirt. Hannah stepped away and waved.

With an answering wave, he slowed and pulled up in front of the long metal barn.

She caught sight of a straw cowboy hat and muscled arm on the passenger side of the truck.

Todd got out, and the other man joined him.

Hannah's eyes widened. The good-looking guy was sure tall for a bull rider. He was at least five feet, eleven inches and solid muscle. His skin tone and black hair made her wonder if he might be one of the Brazilian riders so prevalent in the PBR. Would he speak English?

Hannah approached, and Todd motioned to his friend. "Hannah, meet Alex Silva. Alex, this is Hannah Quinn."

She reached her hand out to the cowboy. "Pleased to meet you, Alex." His dark eyes held a glint of interest, and her heart beat faster. He had such beautiful, smooth skin. Every feature of his face was perfect. *Shit, I'm staring!*

Alex shook her hand, and with clear English but with a strong accent, said, "Good to meet you, Hannah."

She said, "So, I hear you know how to drive a tractor. I have an old John Deere 4550. Will that be a problem?"

Alex grinned. "No problem. I drive tractors very good."

Her father walked up, and she introduced him. "Alex, this is my dad, Ross Harrison. He's visiting from Wyoming." She chewed her lip. May as well get the hard part over. "How much do I need to pay you?"

The corner of his mouth quirked up. "Pay me what you want. I'm here until the season starts, then I ride again."

She drew her brows together and chewed her lip some more. The guy was gimpy. She'd have to take it easy on him. And she couldn't afford much. "How does ten bucks an hour sound?"

He nodded. "Okay. I start tomorrow?"

Hannah looked at her dad. "Maybe you can show him the ropes around here. Would you mind?"

"Sure, honey. That's a good idea."

Placing her hands on her hips, she said, "Alex, I appreciate this. We work eight to five. See you tomorrow." She turned to her friend. "Todd? Thanks, again."

"Glad it worked out."

Alex tipped his hat, and both men headed to Todd's truck.

Alex's broad shoulders and muscular butt held her full attention as he walked away. A buzz of excitement tickled her, something that hadn't happened in a very long time. What would it be like working with this man? He was certainly polite and well-spoken. Damn, he was good to look at. The guy probably had women all over the country dogging him during the season. The man didn't wear a ring, so she assumed he wasn't married. Why was that? And why in the hell was she noticing? Her husband was barely in his grave. Heaving a deep sigh, she turned away. It didn't feel like she'd just lost her husband. He'd been gone from her heart for ages, leaving it scarred and broken.

Her life had changed, and tomorrow a new chapter started. She was a boss, and her only employee was a sexy cowboy. Lord help her.

Chapter Two

ALEX PUNCHED HIS PHONE off. *"¡Burro!"* His ex-wife, Debra's, phone didn't work—again. Sighing heavily, he shifted restlessly in his seat. He sat in the living room at Todd's watching a recorded PBR event. He shouldn't call Debra dumb. She didn't lack intelligence but was forgetful and totally focused on her singing career, such as it was. But he worried about her scattered-brained frame of mind because it affected his two-year-old daughter. Chloe needed a mom who had her shit together, and that just wasn't happening.

Riding the PBR circuit meant he seldom got to see Chloe but that wasn't from lack of trying. He had wanted his daughter to stay with him last year during the off season. Debra moved every few months for her singing gigs. When he tried to set things up, Debra's phone was dead and stayed that way. Weeks later, she called him from a new pay-as-you-go number and asked him for money. By then, the PBR season had started and it was too late to get Chloe.

He'd explained to Debra, again, how important it was to him that she keep a working phone number. He told her that he had wanted to keep Chloe during his summer break. Debra was surprised and said that she would have liked the time to herself. As she always did, she'd promised to tell him if her number changed.

He shut the TV off and headed into the kitchen.

Becky looked up as he walked in. "Hey there. You hungry?"

Sitting next to her at the long granite bar, he said, "Frustrated. Debra's phone is not working. I'm worried for Chloe."

"Damn that woman. Why can't she tell you when she gets a new phone? You're so generous with her, and she doesn't treat you right."

"If my *maē* was still alive, I would ask Debra if Chloe could live with my mother. My daughter would be taken care of very good. It's hard for Debra to find someone to watch Chloe at night. If she lived with my *maē*, Debra could sing and go where she wants."

Becky washed her hands at the sink. "It's too bad your mom died so young. I know you miss her. But you need to get tougher on Debra. This can't go on. You have rights. How many times did you try to see Chloe, and Debra had moved without telling you, and her phone was turned off? Seriously? If you took her to court, she would be in so much trouble."

"I just feel bad. I travel all the time, and Debra, she has a big responsibility with Chloe. I should be a better dad."

Becky slammed her hand down on the counter. "Bullshit, Alex. You're a good father. You give that woman money like it grows on trees. And you try to visit Chloe. Debra needs to find a job where she stays put or at least stay in close contact with you. This flitting from town to town every few months and not telling you just doesn't cut it."

He frowned. "I worry about Chloe when she is big and school begins. How will that work? Debra must quit singing and live in one place. Will she blame Chloe? Debra is not nice to be with when she is mad."

Becky sucked on her bottom lip, as if considering what she wanted to say.

He said, "I know that face. Tell me."

She sighed. "Didn't Dr. Freeman suggest that you stop riding? This is your second pelvic fracture, and this time you needed surgery. And you hated using that walker. Then there's your arm. It's tough to come back from a break to your riding arm, and this was a really bad break."

Taking his hand, she said, "You've been saving up for a ranch of your own for years. Why don't you do that? Buy your own place. Then you can keep Chloe whenever you want. Or, you could go for full custody. It would be a wonderful solution to this mess that Debra makes of Chloe's life."

His stomach had started churning the second Becky mentioned Dr. Tandy Freeman, the head of Sports Medicine for the PBR. No way would Alex consider dropping out of the PBR circuit as the doctor had recommended. Alex still had years of bull riding left in him. Why, look at J. B. Mauney. That guy was as beat up as they come, and he was still riding. No, Alex wouldn't quit. Not yet. There must be some other way to make Chloe's life better.

He pressed his lips together as he considered. "You're right, Becky. Something must change. Chloe needs to be safe."

THE NEXT MORNING, AFTER a quick breakfast, he fixed himself some bean and cheese tacos for lunch and headed off to Hannah's ranch. *Meu Deus, a mulher é bonita.* Yesterday, the sun had streaked her shining copper hair with gold. And those big blue eyes of hers were so fierce when she asked him how much money he wanted. He almost said she shouldn't pay him. She was in a bad way. But the pride in her eyes said *no*. So, he let her name a price. She had something to prove, now that her husband was gone—to herself, if to no one else.

He had something to prove to himself as well. He must be ready to ride by the time the new season started. And he would be. Bull riding was his life, and he wouldn't give it up.

Hannah and her father stepped through the wide barn doors as he pulled up and parked. He waved and got out, walking over to them. "Hi, boss."

Her lips in a firm line, she reached out her hand. "Hey, Alex. My dad is ready to take you around, show you the pastures and the tractor. A guy is coming out here today to fix it. Nobody's driving that thing until it has a new starter. My husband kept saying he'd repair it himself—that we couldn't afford for a mechanic to make a house call." She swallowed and looked out over the pasture for a moment. "Anyway, when it's ready, you'll know which pastures we want to plant, and you can start plowing them. When you're finished, I've got the seed in my other barn."

"Okay." Poor woman. Her husband had died in a terrible way. Alex would treat her gently but without letting her know. She couldn't be more than five feet tall, but something in her eyes told him she was a tough little lady. He followed her father toward the ranch truck and grinned. Alex wouldn't want to get on her bad side.

His thoughts returned to Hannah, time and again, as he learned the ranch with her father. The tiny woman had strength in her, yet her vulnerability was evident in the look of sadness on her face when she wasn't on her guard. He got a strange feeling about her pain and wondered about its true origin. She didn't seem like a woman who had suddenly lost her husband, especially in such a horrible way. Her grief was more fine-tuned, like she'd lived with it for a very long time.

Alex and Ross were driving through one of the desert pastures now. The arid view of the West Texas ranch lacked large trees. It was a wild and lonely land that appealed to his soul. Hannah's father told him that where he would be plowing, they rotated grain crops to preserve the soil's strength and even left the pastures fallow every few years. Careful husbandry was important with the sandy desert soil. Ross was a kind man and very thorough in his explanations. By the time they arrived back at the barn, Alex felt prepared to begin his new job.

Ross led him over to the John Deere which had an obviously-new starter on it. The fateful disc plow was hooked up behind it. Ross said, "It's fixed and ready to go. Why don't you climb aboard, and tell me if you have any questions."

Alex climbed the first two steps and swung the glass door open. The interior was tidy, but dusty. An old pair of leather work gloves sat on the seat. He stepped up the last step and put the gloves on the dash, settling into the cushioned chair. He'd never driven a 4550, but the levers and pedals were obvious in their use. He glanced down at Ross and smiled. "No problem. I can drive it good."

Ross nodded. "I figured. Looks like we're all set, then. I'm glad you're here, Alex. Hannah needs someone on the place, but she's not the kind of person who finds it easy asking for help."

"Don't worry, Mr. Ross. I'll work hard for Hannah."

"I know you will. And, it's just *Ross*, okay?"

Alex grinned. "Okay, Ross."

They turned as Hannah's pickup appeared in a cloud of dust coming down the drive. She pulled up to the barn and stopped. As they walked over, she got out. "Hey, Dad, Alex. How did it go?"

Ross said, "The tractor's fixed, and he knows where to start in the morning."

Alex let his eyes roam over the petite but curvaceous, figure of the woman in front of him. In her worn t-shirt and Wranglers, she wasn't trying to be sexy, but she was. Her face was covered in just the right number of freckles to give her skin a golden glow, and those full lips were a deep pink without a touch of lip color. She had a natural beauty that took his breath away.

Hannah reached out her hand, with her usual all-business expression. "That's great, Alex. I'll see you in the morning, then."

He clasped her small hand, and the calluses on her palm told him just how hard this woman worked. Now that he was here, her life would be easier. "Bye, Hannah."

He strode toward his truck, looking forward to seeing beautiful Hannah in the morning, but not happy at the prospect of the bumping and bouncing his pelvis would experience in the cab of the tractor. Walking was still painful. If he was going to get on the back of a bull soon, his healing would have to be much further along and that worried him. On the bright side, if he could stand the pain the tractor dished out over the next few weeks, maybe getting on the back of a two-thousand-pound bull wouldn't be quite as bad as he expected it to be.

A LITTLE AFTER ELEVEN o'clock that night, his phone rang. Debra's number came up. She must have paid for more minutes. Interesting. Debra usually got a new phone. He answered. "Hey, I called but your phone was off." Loud country music played in the background.

She yelled, "I'm sorry. I'm paid up now. Are you still at Todd's place?"

He pressed the phone to his ear so he could hear better as he hurried into the bathroom and closed the door so he wouldn't wake Chloe. "Yeah, but I got a job at a ranch. The Rocking H. Until I ride bulls again. Where are you now?"

She yelled louder. "I'm in Crowley, just outside of Ft. Worth." She hesitated, then asked, "So, this Rocking H ranch? Is that in Barbwire, too?"

"Yes."

"I have some great news. I'm going to Nashville. I got a gig."

Her voice didn't sound right. He asked, "Are you happy?"

"Of course! It's the break I've been waiting for. Aren't you happy for me, too?"

"Yes. Sure." There was something else going on. "How is Chloe?"

"She's great. She's such a sweet little thing. You hardly know she's there."

Huh? That's not how he remembered his daughter. She got into everything the last time he saw her. But she was precious, all the same. "She's a sweetheart."

"Oh, she is. I have to go. My next set is starting. Nice talking to you, Alex."

He laid the phone on the night stand and turned over. That was the strangest conversation. She didn't even ask him for money. What the hell was going on?

ALEX FOUND HIMSELF looking forward to seeing Hannah as he drove to the Rocking H the next morning. All he knew about the woman was that she lost her husband last week in a horrible accident with a tractor. Did she have children? If she did, he hadn't seen any sign of them.

She appeared sad, but more than that, she seemed angry somehow. He couldn't figure that one out. There was much more to this woman than what he currently knew, and he wanted to find out everything about her. The aura of heartbreak around her drew him in, and not just because of her beauty. Her self-contained strength and fierce sense of independence came through loud and clear. He wished the two of them could work side-by-side, but the best way to help Hannah right now was to get her wheat planted.

Like most ranchers around Barbwire, Hannah grew her crops under dryland conditions, without irrigation, depending on the infrequent rainfall to make them grow. It was a gamble, but water was hard to come by in the desert region, and Hannah, like many people, had no choice. For this reason, planting her wheat in September, just a few short weeks away, was critical. Her crops would take advantage of the fall rains and cooler temperatures while their roots grew deep.

Hannah stepped out of the barn holding a bucket as he pulled in and parked. He walked over to her, his chest tightening with desire. Clearing his throat, he smiled at her, tamping down on his reaction. "Hey, boss. Need help?"

"Hey, Alex. Sure, maybe you can help me feed in the mornings before you set out for the fields." She gestured toward the barn. "They've been fed, but you could throw some cubes in the feeder on the other side of the barn."

"Okay." Hannah didn't smile much, and he had a feeling that had been the case even before she lost her husband.

He finished and headed over to join her at the barn. "Do you have a problem with javelinas digging in your wheat fields?"

"Yep, I sure do. Damn things. They're not like feral hogs. There's a season on javelinas. I have to grit my teeth and let them destroy my wheat. It's so unfair. I should be able to protect my crops."

"That's bad."

She huffed. "Tell me about it." As she headed for her truck, she called over her shoulder. "If I don't see you this afternoon, it'll be in the morning."

He raised his hand. "Sure." As he watched her walk away, his body responded with tingles of desire again. How could it not? Her tight, rounded butt and swinging hips were everything a man could want. Her t-shirt did nothing to hide her full, taut breasts, either. *Meu deus, estou perdido.* My God, he was lost. How was he supposed to keep his eyes off her?

Chapter Three

SEVERAL WEEKS LATER, Hannah glanced again down the long drive to the barn, expecting to see Alex's truck barreling down the road in a cloud of dust. She loved the new feeding routine. It'd been so long since anyone helped her with chores. It took no time at all to feed the stock now. A quiet man, Alex didn't talk unless he had something important to say, and even then, he didn't speak much. Yet, he communicated well. She liked him, and he appeared to care for her, too.

He did an amazing job on plowing the pastures. In another couple of days, he could start planting. On the Rocking H, they grew all their own hay and used the wheat for grazing as well. So, she must grow successful crops and couldn't miss out on the soon-to-come fall rains.

An engine rumbled in the distance as Alex sped up the drive. She grinned to herself. That man sure got here in a hurry every morning.

After he parked, he walked over to her. "How are you, boss?"

Used to his teasing address now, she said, "Your boss is fine. I'm driving to Carlsbad for some shopping today, so I won't be around. Call me if you need anything."

They set about their feeding routine and finished quickly. Alex stopped her before she could leave. "Hannah, may I ask you something? Before you say yes, it's personal."

Her heart thumped her chest wall, and she found it hard to breathe. With her fragile control, she avoided personal conversations. To her surprise, she heard herself say, "Go ahead."

He took a deep breath and exhaled. "I'm sorry, Hannah. Please, don't be angry. I think we are friends now, and I want to understand. I feel your pain. But maybe this is an old pain, not from your husband?"

At his unexpected words, she took a step back. He'd looked into her soul.

Then she got mad. How the hell did he know whether she grieved or not? Gritting her teeth, she said, "You don't know anything about me or my feelings. But, you're right about one thing. I'm sure you'll hear around town. Ty had an affair before he was killed. So, yeah, I quit loving him long before he died." Biting her lower lip to keep it from trembling, she spun around and stalked to her truck.

Furious, she gunned the engine, speeding down the drive. *Shit, why did Alex stick his nose in my business? He spoiled everything.*

Eventually, she turned on to Highway 285 and set her cruise control. Calmer now that she'd had time to think, her angry reaction didn't make sense. Gazing at the empty desert landscape stretching into the distance, she asked herself, *Do I feel guilty because I'm not sad? Am I a bad person because I didn't love my husband when he died?* Of course, wishing him dead had never entered her mind, but his death left her numb, nothing more. His mean, blaming words about her infertility and his callous flouting of his affair had shattered her love into a million pieces, leaving her nothing to mourn the man with.

So why did she get so angry with Alex for pointing that out? No one else had guts enough to bring her lack of grief up to her. Maybe she should be grateful he'd made her face it. If nothing else, she owed the man an apology.

SHE DIDN'T GET HOME until evening, and Alex left at five. After she put her purchases away and took a bath, she sat on the couch and dialed his number. When he picked up, she said, "Hey, employee."

He laughed. "Hey, boss. How was Carlsbad?"

"The usual. I'm exhausted. Listen ..." Unsure what to say, she paused.

"Yes, boss?"

"I'm sorry I jumped on you. I don't know why I got so angry. You're right, I'm not like a regular widow. My husband really hurt me this past year. I'm overwhelmed and kind of lost. But not sad."

"Hannah, I'm your friend. I hope you know that."

Her best friend, Lucy, moved to Dallas a few years ago, and Hannah missed having her close by. "Thanks, Alex."

"Maybe sometime you will tell me what makes you sad, huh?"

Sighing, she said, "Bye, Alex. I'll see you in the morning."

She suddenly felt better than she had all day. *Whiskey, here I come.* Throwing two ice cubes in a glass, she poured herself three fingers of Maker's Mark and took a lingering sip. *That hits the spot.* She grabbed some empty boxes out of the garage and headed to her closet, dumping everything of Ty's into them. Most of his clothes were in town, but she boxed up what was left and anything else she could find. She kept his guns, though. The two of them had made wills. His stuff went to her, anyway. She'd shoved his pictures in drawers ages ago, so she dug them out and dumped them in the boxes, too.

When she finished, she stared at a sad testament to her marriage. Shocked that Ty had already moved out so many of his belongings, it made her angry, but, at last, it also made her cry.

She texted his mother, whom she hadn't spoken to in months, even at the funeral. Neither of them knew what to say in the face of Ty's blatant affair.

> *I collected some of Ty's things. I'll bring them by and leave them on the porch tomorrow. I hope you're doing okay. I'm so sorry for your loss.*

Then she dragged the boxes to the garage.

As she sank down on the couch, a sense of freedom settled over her. The pain of the past year hurt less with Ty and his things gone. She accepted that it was okay to be happy that the man who had damaged her so terribly wouldn't hurt her anymore.

She fixed one last glass of whiskey. A harder task lay ahead of her. Finally talking to her parents about her husband had revealed something about herself. It wasn't just Ty who blamed her for being infertile. She desperately wanted a child and hated her body for letting her down. Somehow, some way, she must deal with that. Or, it would destroy her.

SEVERAL DAYS LATER, as Hannah stared into her cabinet hoping for dinner inspiration, her phone rang, and she didn't recognize the number. "Hello?"

"Hannah? This is Becky, Todd's wife?"

Huh? Becky never called her. "Hi. How are you?"

"Honey, I was just wondering if you would come to dinner Saturday evening? Todd's barbequing in the back yard, and I'm making all the fixings to go with it. It'll be great. Won't you please come?"

It had been a long time since she'd gone anywhere. But, why not? She liked Becky. "I'd love to. What can I bring?"

"Just yourself. I'm so glad you're coming, honey. Is six o'clock okay?"

"It's just fine, Becky. I'll see you Saturday." When Hannah hung up, she found her pulse thrumming in anticipation. But, God, what would she wear? She never wore anything but t-shirts and jeans. Damn. If she'd known, she could have bought something new in Carlsbad.

She went through her closet, hanger by hanger, and sighed. She only found t-shirts, and worn-out, at that. Unless she counted her funeral dress and winter shirts. She had some things packed away that harked back to the first carefree years of her marriage, before her body let her down. Before her husband betrayed her. No way would she ever wear that stuff again. She'd drag that box to the garage tomorrow, too.

Flopping on the bed, she closed her eyes and wished she'd never agreed to go. Why didn't she think before she opened her mouth? Two seconds would have told her she probably didn't have anything to wear. Forget the t-shirts. Her jeans were all worn and faded, some even torn. No amount of starch would make them respectable.

If Lucy still lived here, she could borrow clothes from her. But Hannah had all but lost contact with her friend in the past year. So deep in a fog of depression, Hannah didn't reach out to anyone, even her best friend. And she ignored most of Lucy's calls, unable to face talking. She'd sent a text to her friend after Ty's death and told Lucy she'd call her when she felt she could discuss it.

Snuggling into the comfort of her bed, she prepared for the first honest conversation with Lucy in a very long time. When she answered, Hannah said, "It's your long-lost bestie calling. Can you talk?"

"Are you kidding? You're all I can think about these days. I wanted to call you so badly, but I know when you say you'll call, that you don't want to talk. How are you, honey?"

Hearing Lucy's voice lifted an enormous weight from Hannah's shoulders. "I'm sorry, Lucy. I should have gotten in touch, and I should have answered when you phoned me. I'm a mess and haven't been a very good friend."

"I love you. Don't worry about it. Tell me, how are you? How are you managing things right now?"

"I'm actually ..." It sounded horrible to say that she was feeling good, but it was the truth. Hell, Lucy would understand if Hannah explained. "Lucy, I'm better than I have been in a long time." She went on to tell her about packing Ty's belongings, hiring Alex, and her new sense of freedom from the pain of the past year.

Lucy said, "Honey, good for you. I'm going to speak ill of the dead. That bastard treated you bad, and you have every right to be happy that he's out of your life. I know you didn't want him to die, but that's the way it is. He talked awful to you, blaming you because you couldn't have babies. If I'd been a man, I would have beat his ass."

Hannah giggled. "Thanks, Lucy. I love you." After catching up on Lucy's life for a few minutes, Hannah ended the call. Closing her eyes, she enjoyed the warmth of the sun's rays shining through the bedroom window. Like the sun, her heart had begun to glow after a long, bleak year of darkness.

With new determination, she decided to take an evening trip to Carlsbad the next day. What else did she have to do with her nights? It was time to buy some new clothes for the new her.

Alex had never seen her dressed up. Tingles rippled up her belly. Was it bad that she wanted to look pretty for him? She stood and peered in the dresser mirror. It had been a long time since she'd examined herself. She'd turn thirty next year—were those crow's feet starting at the corners of her eyes? She leaned closer. Nope, but, damn, she better start using moisturizer. That went on her list too.

Heading into the kitchen to set up coffee for the next morning, her thoughts returned to Alex. The handsome cowboy sure kept her mind busy lately. She imagined his lopsided smile and the intense look in his dark eyes when he spoke to her. Her nipples hardened, and she sucked in a breath. Damn, she'd definitely been too long without a man.

Chapter Four

THURSDAY MORNING, ALEX stacked the empty bucket in the barn and headed outside. Hannah stood waiting for him. They both turned as the sound of an engine came from far down the ranch drive. A cloud of dust approached. He said, "You expecting someone?"

"Nope. You?"

"No."

He waited, and the dust drew closer. A vehicle emerged, and he pulled his brows together. It couldn't be. Glancing at Hannah, he said, "I think I know who this is, but I don't understand why she's here." He started walking, anxiety flooding his stomach with acid.

The old sedan slowed, coming to a stop next to him. The window rolled down and he rested his hands on it. "Debra? Is Chloe okay? How did you find me?"

With a flashy smile, she pushed the door open and stepped out of the car. "Hi, baby, I found you!" She threw her arms around his neck and hugged him.

He glanced back at Hannah.

She stared at the performance, expressionless.

Pulling Debra's arms from his neck, he bent to look inside the car. "How is Chloe? What is happening, Debra? Why are you here?"

Pouting, she said, "What? I need a reason to come see you?"

He sighed. "You never come to see me. Tell me, what is wrong?"

Angry now, she yanked open the back door and unstrapped Chloe from her car seat. "I told you I have a gig in Nashville." Pulling her daughter into her arms, she hugged her and thrust the little girl at Alex. "Now it's your turn. I can't take care of her anymore. I need to focus on my career. You're her daddy. You take her now." Relieved of Chloe, Debra pulled two small pink suitcases from the car and plopped them down in the dust.

Panic rose to his throat, and he swallowed hard. "Debra, I'll be riding soon. When will you be back?"

"I don't know. I may not be back. She's yours now. You figure it out. I've done it all on my own long enough."

"On your own? I help you. Debra, you can't do this."

She shrugged and yanked loose the belt that held the car seat, taking it out and dropping it on the ground. Slamming the door, she got back behind the wheel. "I'm doing it. You'll be fine. You've got *daddy* written all over you." Throwing the car in reverse, she spun the car around and sped back down the drive.

Chloe, who had been quiet through Debra's tirade, began to cry as she watched her mother leave.

Alex snuggled her close, patting her back. "*Meu bebê menina.*" Bouncing his baby girl up and down, he left her bags where they were and walked over to Hannah. "This is terrible. Debra has abandoned her. I don't know what to do."

Chloe's crying faded, and she whimpered, finally becoming quiet and limp in his arms. As he patted her back, his mind worked furiously on the problem. He wanted to help Hannah, but he couldn't work and take care of his baby girl, too. "I'm sorry. When I said I would help you, I didn't know I would have my *bebê*."

Hannah bit her lip, looking steadily at his daughter. "Alex, I'll watch her today while you finish plowing the last field. We'll figure something out. I've got to get my wheat planted. Does that work for you?"

He expelled a long breath. It gave him time to figure out what the hell he would do with his precious little girl. Now that he'd had a couple of minutes to get used to the idea, he was happy.

Knowing it always made her giggle, he tugged on a lock of Chloe's long curly hair.

She turned her head, and her big blue eyes met his.

"*Meu bebê*, this nice lady is Hannah. She will take care of you while I work. I'll come back tonight. Mommy is far away. You will live with Daddy now."

Chloe stared at him. The poor little thing was so used to bouncing from one stranger to another while her mom sang, he figured this was nothing new to her. He hugged Chloe to him again. He'd give her a stable home, at least for now. God knew what would happen when it came time for him to ride again. He wouldn't think that far ahead. Right now, he must find a way to make the next few weeks work.

He handed his limp daughter over to Hannah. "Her name is Chloe. She can use the toilet. Thanks for your help. I'll talk to Todd. I hope to find something else for tomorrow."

Hannah's smiled gently as she cuddled the little girl in her arms. "We'll be okay. She can ride around with me today, and

I'll work on my books after lunch so she can take a nap. We'll make out."

Hannah had eyes only for Chloe, and he smiled as he walked to his truck. His daughter would be fine with his boss for this one day. He glanced in his rear-view mirror as he drove off, and Hannah was placing his daughter's car seat in her truck. Despite the flutter of anxiety in his belly at his new responsibility, this was a good thing. He could now get to know his beautiful little daughter.

HANNAH PEEKED AT THE stoic little girl in the passenger side of her truck. She didn't speak, nor did she meet Hannah's eyes. That was okay. The tiny thing's life had just been turned upside down. Lord, she was gorgeous. Those kinky, curly curls, which were kind of medium brown, and her huge blue eyes radiated the essence of beautiful innocence. Hannah wanted to squeeze her and never let her go.

Hannah turned to her window as her chest tightened. She needed to let her go, though. She couldn't get attached to this sad little thing. If her mother didn't come snatch her back, Alex would take her away when the next PBR season started. God, she couldn't fall in love with this baby, no matter what. Her heart couldn't take losing a child. No, Hannah had to keep her distance. She took a quick look at the little girl, and Chloe stared back at her. Damn, how could she resist the little thing?

Hannah smiled and said, "Are you hungry, honey?"

Chloe nodded slowly.

"We'll stop by the house and make a snack. I'm kind of hungry too."

Tucking her lips inside her mouth, Chloe stared at Hannah.

Does she even talk? Maybe she's behind for her age. Alex should know. Hannah pulled into the driveway at the ranch house and waited for the dust to settle. "This is where I live. I'll unbuckle you, and we can find something to eat."

Hannah got out and opened the passenger door.

Chloe fiddled with her harness.

"Let me help you with that, sweetie." Freeing the child, she pulled her into her arms, and Chloe clung to her this time. God, it felt amazing. Chloe's fragile little bones hardly had any meat on them. What had that damn woman been feeding her, anyway? *Hold on, Hannah, don't be so judgey. The girl might be a picky eater.* "Here we go, now. First, we'll both go potty. Then we'll eat."

Just in case Alex had been wrong about Chloe's toileting prowess, Hannah went first, setting an example. But she needn't have worried. As soon as she set Chloe on the toilet seat, the little girl let fly with a steady stream of urine. The poor thing had really needed to go. Good for her for holding it so long. Hannah pulled some paper off the roll. "Do you need help with this?"

Chloe slowly nodded assent.

Hannah took care of it, and they both washed their hands. Carrying the little girl to the kitchen, she asked, "Do you like ham sandwiches?"

Chloe rolled her lips inside her mouth.

Hannah got the idea this was her response when she felt unsure or shy. "How about peanut butter and jelly. Do you like that?"

She nodded.

"Right, that's what we'll have. And some chips and milk."

A few minutes later, when Hannah set food in front of the little girl, she moved at a speed that had been lacking since she arrived at the ranch. Her first bite was huge, washed down with a gulp of milk. The child must have been starving.

Hannah's heart clenched and she stared at her plate so that Chloe couldn't see her pity. As Hannah well knew, everyone needed their pride.

Chloe finished quickly and looked at Hannah.

"Would you like some more?"

"No."

She could talk! "Okay, honey. We'll come back here for lunch later. We can eat some more then."

Eating seemed to have broken a spell. The rest of the morning, though she spoke in monosyllables, Chloe answered when spoken to. Hannah thrilled at the sound of her soft little voice. A sharp ache deep inside of Hannah softened at the edges. She couldn't keep her hands off the little girl. Every few minutes, she was either smoothing her untamed hair, clasping her small hand, or patting her frail-seeming back.

At lunch time, they drove back to the house. This time she did fix ham sandwiches, cutting the meat up in small pieces so it would be easy to eat before putting it on the bread.

Chloe loved it, gobbling her sandwich down.

My God, wasn't the child ever fed? Hannah's picky-eater theory was going down the tube. This baby girl needed food. Hannah pulled an apple out of the fridge and cut it up. "I love apples. I'll bet you do, too."

As soon as it appeared on her plate, Chloe picked up a piece of apple and crunched into it, smiling for the first time.

That smile did something to Hannah. Ripples of pure joy swept through her, something she hadn't felt in a very long time. *Oh God, how can I not become attached to this precious child?* Tears pooled in Hannah's eyes, and she strode to the sink, hiding her face. All she'd ever wanted was a child like this, and that woman discarded her like an old pair of shoes.

Fury filled Hannah's chest, and she clutched the cabinet. It was so damned unfair. *Why? Why did her body fail her in this?* Biting her lip until she couldn't stand the pain, she forced the useless thought from her mind. She wouldn't go back to that dark misery again. She splashed her face with cold water and dried it with a paper towel. Enough self-pity. She could enjoy Chloe for weeks to come. Somehow, she also had to protect her heart.

HANNAH DROVE BACK TO the barn at four thirty and took Chloe out of the truck. Still holding the little girl, Hannah said, "I have to feed all these cows. Do you think you can walk with me while I do that?"

Chloe's eyes opened wide, yet she nodded slowly.

"You're very brave." Hannah set her on the ground. "Now you hold on right here." She handed the little girl the hem of her t-shirt and walked into the barn with Chloe at her side. Filling a bucket with cow cubes, she walked toward the pen beside the barn. "Don't let go now. We're going inside."

Chloe scrunched a bigger handful of Hannah's shirt into her fist but didn't lag behind.

The cows heard Hannah open the gate and headed in their direction. She said, "Don't worry, Chloe, it'll take them a while to get over here." Hannah held the bucket down low when they got to the feeder. "Why don't you grab some cubes and dump them in there."

Chloe reached inside and grabbed two of the big cow cubes, dropping them in the metal feeder, looking pleased with herself.

Hannah slung the cubes all through the long feeder, plucking Chloe into her arms as the first hungry cow barged in and ducked her head into the feed.

From her safe perch, Chloe eyed the cows with interest. Hannah headed back to the gate. "You're a good helper, and a very brave one, too." Without thinking, she pressed a quick kiss to Chloe's cheek.

Chloe stared at her.

Hannah asked, "Do you remember my name?"

Chloe shook her head.

"I'm Hannah. You can call me Hannah, okay?"

Chloe nodded.

"You tell me when you need something, and I'll help you, honey."

The two of them had just finished feeding when Alex drove up.

He jumped out as soon as he put the truck in park. "Thank you, Hannah. I'm so sorry."

Hannah picked up Chloe, her stomach suddenly in knots. "You have nothing to be sorry about, Alex. Chloe was wonderful today. I was able to take care of everything I had planned." She turned to Chloe. "We were just fine, weren't we?"

Chloe opened her mouth and looked from Hannah to her father, then sucked on her fingers.

Pressing Chloe's face to her chest, Hannah said, "It's okay, baby, you don't need to answer." She looked Alex in the eyes. "I'd be glad to take care of Chloe during the day. It won't be a problem. She even helped me feed tonight. She's smart and knows how to take directions. She's potty-trained and took a good nap today. I don't see any reason why it won't work out." Hannah's pulse raced, every muscle in her body tense.

He narrowed his eyes. "Are you sure, Hannah? Taking care of Chloe is a lot of work. You're busy."

She let out a breath. "I'm sure. We got along great. And it's not forever, right?" Saying that sent a knife-like pain through her chest. Damn, what was she doing getting so involved? Gusting out a sigh, she decided she didn't care. All she knew was this little girl was hers. At least for now.

Alex shrugged. "Okay. Thank you, Hannah. I'll bring her in the morning." He held out his arms. "Come here, *bebê*."

As Chloe's little arm slid from Hannah's neck, aching need settled in her heart. *Shit. Shit. Shit. I'm already too attached.* She stepped back woodenly and turned away. "I'll see you to-morrow, Alex." Unable to watch the child drive away, she headed into the barn. In the next fifteen hours she'd better get it to-gether. If she didn't, she was lost.

Chapter Five

HANNAH HAD LOVED SPENDING the past few days with Chloe, and telling her goodbye Friday afternoon had been hard. By noon on Saturday, she missed the little girl something awful. The only thing that gave her solace was the fact that she would see her at six at the barbeque.

Yesterday, after Alex drove off with his daughter, Hannah had headed to Carlsbad and bought clothes, and not just for the barbeque. Her wardrobe now contained several blouses, new t-shirts and jeans, a beautiful straw Stetson, since her current one looked like something the cat drug in, and she even bought a dress.

But those purchases weren't what excited Hannah. While in the western store buying her Wranglers, she bought some tiny jeans, teensy boots and socks, and several t-shirts that would fit Chloe's little frame. Though the girl's mother had dropped her off with two small suitcases, when Alex opened them, they held mostly blankets and stuffed animals. Chloe desperately needed clothes.

Hannah finished repairing the fence a cow ran through that morning, and by the time she got back to the house she needed to get ready. Her pulse picked up speed as she anticipated seeing Alex. The past few days, while watching him with Chloe, her attraction had grown. He adored his daughter, holding her with tender hands and speaking to her in such a gentle voice.

So, she took care with her appearance, even wearing make-up and curling her long hair. Inspecting herself in the mirror, she admired the new turquoise blouse which set off the color of her copper curls. Her concealer helped cover the dark circles under her eyes. After adding some turquoise earrings, she grabbed her purse.

Surprised, she found herself nervous on the ride to Todd's place. Would Alex think she'd dressed to impress him? Actually, she had, but she was his boss, how embarrassing if he figured it out. Wouldn't she have dressed special anyway, if it had just been Todd and Becky? Biting her lip, she considered that one. The answer was *probably*, so she was okay.

Becky came out to greet Hannah when she drove up, and called, "Hi there. Come on in."

Hannah grabbed the gift bag and her purse and stepped out of the truck, her pulse picking up speed. This was her first time to visit Todd and his family. They lived in a long, low ranch house with tan siding, perfect for their desert surroundings. "Hi, Becky. I brought some things for Chloe."

"Everyone's out back." Becky gave Hannah a hug and led her through the house which had a distinctive western flair.

She loved the wood-burned horseshoes on the pine furniture and the brightly-colored Mexican blankets thrown over the backs of the couch and chairs.

When they got to the kitchen, Becky said, "Hannah, this is my son, Charlie."

A small boy of about five put out his hand, "Hi."

Somehow, she'd forgotten that Todd and Becky had a boy. She clasped his hand. "Hi, Charlie." He was a real cutie.

Stepping out the back door, Hannah's gaze sought Chloe, finding her playing with a black-and-white border collie. Hannah headed in the little girl's direction, kneeling down in front of her and giving her a hug.

Alex called, "Hello, Hannah. Would you like a beer?"

Her vision zeroed in on his broad chest and every muscle that bulged through the thin material covering it. *Oh my God. He's wearing a t-shirt.* Was her tongue hanging out? "Hey, Alex, yeah, I'd love one." She ripped her gaze away from the sexy Brazilian and released the child, heading over to her host. Licking her suddenly-dry lips, she said, "Hi, Todd. What's on the menu?"

"Here on the pit we have deer sausage links and some steaks. Becky's making beans and cornbread and some potato salad. We have iced tea, too." He eyed her and grinned. "Don't you look pretty, Miss Hannah. I'm glad you came."

Alex walked over and handed her a beer. "You're beautiful, Hannah." He smiled and the spark in those big brown eyes of his had her insides turning to mush.

"Thanks, guys." She popped her beer open and took a sip, keeping her eyes on Todd and away from oh-so-gorgeous Alex. That's when she remembered she held Chloe's present.

Scrupulously keeping her gaze on Alex's face, she said, "I hope you don't mind. I bought some things for Chloe when I was in town last night. Now that she's my helper, I thought she should dress the part."

He smiled. "Sure, Hannah. Thank you."

Her duty to Todd finished, she couldn't wait to get her hands on the little girl again. She called, "Chloe, I have a present for you."

Chloe seemed confused.

Alex said, "Come here, *bebê*," as he and Hannah walked toward the child.

Chloe stood uncertainly, smiling at her dad. "Birthday, Daddy?"

"No, *bebê*, you just had your birthday."

Hannah knelt in front of her again and handed Chloe the bag, which was nearly as tall as the little girl. "Pull out those papers, honey."

Her clear blue eyes wide with excitement, Chloe threw the brightly-colored tissue on the grass and peered inside. "Shoes?"

Bright red boots sat on top of the clothes. Hannah said, "Yes, you have your own cowgirl boots now. Let's see what else is in there." Hannah gave Chloe the boots and brought out the tiny Wranglers, socks, and cute little t-shirts. One said, *Daddy's Little Cowgirl.*

Alex picked up the shirt. "Aw, *meu bebê menina.*" Wrapping his arm around Hannah's shoulders, he squeezed her in a warm hug. "Thank you, Hannah. My little girl will be a real cowgirl now."

Hannah shivered. His muscular chest pressed into her shoulder as his arm gently embraced her. It had been so long since a man had touched her with tenderness. A raw ache welled inside her, and it was all she could do to keep from leaning into him.

Grinning, Alex said, "We must put this on you, Chloe." He stood and held his hand out to his daughter. "Do you want to wear your jeans and boots, too?"

Chloe nodded eagerly.

Hannah's fingers ached to be the one to dress the precious little thing in her new clothes. But it wasn't her place. Her gaze clung to Alex and Chloe as they disappeared into the house. A light went out inside Hannah. This is how it would always be. It would never be her putting on the clothes because it would never be her child. Picking up her beer, she headed over to a chair and dropped into it. Chugging her beer until she drained the can, she crushed it with one hand. It was time she got used to being barren. How she would do that was a mystery, but she had to try. She lost a whole year living in a black hole of misery and it couldn't go on. The other way out was killing herself, and she was no coward.

She walked over and grabbed a beer from the ice chest, then returned to Todd's side. "Anything I can do to help?"

"Naw, I've got this." He smiled. "How are you, Hannah? You holding up?"

She stared at her boots. People expected her to be grieving.

He said, "Look, Ty was an asshole. I don't know how he could do that to you. Just so you know, I didn't approve. I told him so, too."

Surprised, she looked up. "You did?"

"Damn sure did, and I told that woman he was with that she should be ashamed of herself."

Hannah grinned and bit her lip. "Thanks, Todd. I didn't know people had my back."

"Hell, yes. A lot of us disapproved. You didn't deserve what he did to you."

A weight lifted from her. Instead of thinking she was stupid, her neighbors had cared about how badly Ty had treated her. She hadn't really been alone after all. Taking a sip of beer, she smiled to herself as a sense of wellness filled up her insides. "Todd?

He glanced up from the grill.

"Thanks for inviting me."

Grinning, he patted her back. "You're welcome, Hannah. I'm just glad you said yes. We should have asked you over a long time ago."

The back door opened, and Alex came out holding a transformed Chloe. The little girl's face held the widest smile Hannah had ever seen on her, and she swung her booted legs back and forth. Alex called, "Look at my little cowgirl, Hannah."

She was by his side before she realized she was moving, her arms outstretched for Chloe. "Can I hold you, baby?"

Chloe leaned toward Hannah, and she scooped the little girl into her arms. *Oh God. She feels so good.* Hannah, her eyes closed, hugged the little girl, moving slowly side-to-side.

Alex spoke, interrupting her communion. "Hannah, can I ask you a favor? My daughter must have more clothes, and you know Carlsbad. Would you help me buy some for her?"

Her heart leapt. She had a fantasy about shopping for children's clothes. "Of course. There's Wal-Mart and also a mall. How about next Saturday afternoon?"

He smiled. "Thank you, Hannah. What time? I'll pick you up."

"About three?"

"Okay. I'll buy dinner, too." He paused a moment, and touched Hannah's arm. "I appreciate everything you do for me and Chloe." His eyes held Hannah's for an extra moment.

She felt the warmth from his gaze swirling in her chest, growing hotter. The man was so sweet and, damn, he was sexy. And the guy wasn't even trying. "You're welcome. I enjoy my time with Chloe. Honestly."

Chloe had been inspecting Hannah's dangling earrings and said, "Pwetty."

Hannah couldn't bear to put the child down, so carried her over by Becky, who had brought out a pot of beans to the long wooden picnic table in the shade on the porch. "I'm sorry, I should have been inside helping you."

"Oh my gosh. No way. You're here to visit and have a good time. I love the clothes you bought Chloe. She's adorable in them. That was so kind of you."

Hannah kissed the little girl's cheek and hugged her again. "She's my helper. She needed to dress the part, and I couldn't help noticing that she could use a few new things."

Becky said, "Chloe, honey, why don't you come inside, and I'll give you a couple of cookies and some milk."

In the kitchen, Hannah sat the little girl in the booster seat at the table while Becky set out the cookies.

Becky motioned for Hannah to follow her into the living room. Narrowing her eyes, she shook her head and said, "I swear, if I get my hands on Debra ... if you knew how much money Alex gives that woman, you'd want to kill her, too. She's sure not spending it on Chloe." Becky told Hannah about the circumstances of Alex's marriage and divorce, adding, "Some men would send a check because the court made them and forget about the kid. Alex isn't like that, though. When Debra found out she was pregnant and insisted that she could prove it was his, they were already in the middle of their divorce. Alex immediately offered child support and had the papers changed to include it. He didn't even wait for the DNA results, which his lawyer requested. And he's always wanted to be a part of Chloe's life. Something Debra makes damn hard."

Hannah frowned. "She doesn't sound like a very good mother. Poor Chloe." Acid poured into Hannah's stomach. What if the woman came back and took her daughter away from Alex? Pulse pounding, Hannah asked, "Has Alex ever tried to do something about the way Debra lives?"

Becky made a rude noise. "He makes excuses for her and says Debra has it hard, raising Chloe as a single mom, which is such bullshit. I told you how he throws money at her. Chloe should have decent clothes, and Debra could hire a nanny if she needed help. But she won't stay anywhere long enough to make things right for Chloe. As it is, she scrounges anyone she can find to watch Chloe at night."

Hannah reached for the back of the couch, feeling light-headed. This baby could *not* go back to those living conditions. Surely Alex would do something about it if, or when, Debra came back. "I hope Alex will make some changes this time. Chloe needs him to stand up for her."

Becky pressed her lips together. "I couldn't agree more."

They filed back into the kitchen, and Hannah sat next to Chloe. "You like those cookies, honey?"

She nodded, her mouth full.

Hannah's heart twisted. She had to protect this vulnerable little girl. How, she wasn't sure.

Later, after a wonderful dinner, Alex walked Hannah to her truck, holding his daughter in his arms. "I'm glad you came, Hannah."

Before she could open her door, he smiled at her, looking into her eyes. "I want to hug you. Is that okay?"

Her heart leapt. The corner of her mouth ticked up nervously. "Sure."

His arm slid around her and she leaned into him, loving that Chloe's little arm went around her neck. He said, "I like you, Hannah. You're a nice person. And my *bebê* likes you, too." Alex held his embrace for a long moment, and let her go. "Drive safely. We will see you Monday morning."

Hannah lifted Chloe's hand to her lips and kissed it. "See you, honey." As she drove off, she could still feel the warmth of Alex's embrace. It was wonderful and exciting and terrifying. But she couldn't get attached to this amazing man. He'd be gone in a couple of months. She wouldn't be stupid with her heart again.

THAT NIGHT, ALEX LAY with his head on his arms as Hannah filled his thoughts.

In the darkness, Chloe turned over in her playpen at the foot of his bed.

His *bebê* was a restless sleeper—one reason she wasn't in his bed. That thought reminded him that he was alone tonight, as usual. He wasn't a saint. Sometimes, on the road, he took a buckle bunny to his hotel room. All the unmarried guys did. It wasn't his thing, though, and he didn't do it often. Hannah would never be a buckle bunny. The more he worked with her, the more he admired her.

He had asked Todd about her husband, learning all about the jerk's heartless infidelity. Hannah didn't deserve that. Unconsciously, Alex's hand balled into a fist. Too bad Hannah didn't have a brother to stand up for her. Todd told him about that, too. If Alex had known, he would have done something about her asshole husband and probably been thrown in jail for the first time in his life.

He was only getting to know Hannah, but he knew himself too well. He cared for her—as more than just a friend. His heart went out to her because he sensed her pain. His body responded to her sexy beauty. His intellect admired her strength of will. She was an amazing woman, and he wanted her.

Hannah had a way about her that said *keep your distance*. Somehow, he had to break through that if he were to learn the cause of her sadness. Her husband had hurt her terribly. It wouldn't be easy. And patience wasn't something he was good at. He'd be riding again in a very short time. He had to make the weeks ahead count. His primary goal must be to help Hannah. A woman shouldn't be so sad. If he could do that before the next season started, he would be happy. Getting the stubborn little woman to open up would be hard. But he was a bull rider, and bull riders love a challenge.

Chapter Six

HANNAH SEARCHED THROUGH the tiny outfits at Wal-Mart, glancing at Alex as his fingers skipped through the hangers on a rack not far from her. His intense preoccupation with his search was so sweet it made her heart ache. He wanted to buy a new wardrobe for his daughter, and they were looking for sleepwear as well as play clothes that would stand up to the West Texas dirt.

Alex surprised her when he showed up this afternoon without Chloe. He said that she would get tired before they got home, so he'd left her with Becky.

He held up a pink two-piece shorts outfit. "*Hannah, este é muito precioso, sim?*"

She grinned. He sometimes lapsed into Portuguese when he got excited, but it didn't take much to figure out that he thought the outfit was precious. "I like it. She'll look adorable."

Grinning, he put the set in his basket.

She eyed him as he searched the next rack with the same intensity as before. He was such a wonderful father. Chloe was a lucky little girl in that respect. Maybe her mother did try, but her lifestyle didn't allow Debra to provide a good home for her daughter. Hannah worried desperately about Chloe if the woman came back. Debra still retained custody, despite the fact that she dumped her daughter in Alex's lap with no warning.

Out of the corner of her eye, Hannah noted Alex dropping several more outfits in his basket. Wandering over, she asked, "Do you think you have enough play clothes? I have four sets of pajamas for her. If you're through here, maybe we can go to the mall and look for a few little dresses." *Please let him agree. I'm dying to see Chloe in a dress.*

"Sure. I'll pay." He dropped Hannah's things into his basket.

While he was at the register, she put her cart away, realizing how much fun she had shopping with him. Around Alex, she relaxed and enjoyed herself in a way that she couldn't remember doing in a very long time. With him, she forgot she was barren Hannah, the woman who would always be alone.

Alex grabbed his bags and pushed his empty basket into the row beside her. As he escorted her across the parking lot, he settled his palm lightly in the small of her back.

Little shivers ran up her spine. He made her feel beautiful. Her pulse sped up, and she sucked in a breath, wanting to lean into the man and feel his arms around her. *I'm losing it.* Increasing her pace, she added some distance between them. She could *not* fall for a short-term cowboy. He was here for the season, and then he would be gone.

Alex clicked the locks on his truck as they approached and opened her door for her. "Hop in." He pulled her seatbelt out and handed it to her before she could reach for it.

She loved the way he handled all the tiny details and smiled. "Thanks, Alex."

"My pleasure."

The special light in his eyes when he said it sent butterflies fluttering around in her tummy.

Alex put his purchases in the back seat. "Tell me where this mall is, Hannah. After we buy pretty dresses for Chloe, you will tell me someplace good to eat." He grinned at her as he started the engine.

Alex kept up the conversation as he drove, his dark gaze frequently leaving the road and searching hers. His interest, his warmth, his sweetness—they all drew her in. She was starved for these things he offered her. This irresistible cowboy was a whole heap of trouble headed straight for her heart.

Once at the mall, they found J. C. Penney's. Her secret dream had been to have a little girl to buy tiny dresses for, and tonight fulfilled that dream. Fingering the ruffles and lace on the dresses and imagining Chloe in them transported Hannah to a world of wonder. She lost track of Alex, of the time, of everything.

Suddenly, Alex was beside her, with his hand on her shoulder. "Hannah?"

She blinked and stopped rubbing the tiny pink dress against her cheek. "What?" He held two small dresses in his hand, and she looked at her whole basket full of them. *What was I thinking?*

Alex grinned at her. "I only have one daughter, Hannah. I don't think she can wear all those."

Heat rose to Hannah's face. "I'll put them back. She probably only needs three or four, right?"

Alex stared, his eyes curious. "We can buy more if you like."

Embarrassed, she shook her head. "No, no." As she rushed to make her choices, it was almost unbearable to hang the dresses back on the rack. She'd waited so long for this! "I tell you what, why don't you choose two from this mess, Alex? I need to use the ladies' room. Sorry." Without meeting his eyes, she strode away, not caring where the restrooms were.

When would she realize that Chloe wasn't her child? *Somehow, I've got to start protecting myself.* She sucked in a breath. *God, I don't know how. I want a child!* Tears pooled in her eyes, and now she did want the rest room.

After asking directions, she went in a stall and sat on the commode, not bothering to remove her clothes. She wiped her eyes with tissue. Every time she thought she had a handle on her life, something like this happened, and she realized she was still totally screwed up. Still barren Hannah.

Resting her face in her palms, she breathed deep, hoping to find peace.

THE DOOR OPENED, AND Alex called, "Hannah, are you in here?"

Oh my God! "Yes, I'll be right there."

How long have I been sitting like this? "Shit!" She bit her lip hard. "Dammit! How the hell will you explain this one, Hannah?" With makeup on, she couldn't splash water on her face. She pushed the door open, and there was a very worried Alex, with his bags in his hands, staring at her.

"Hannah, I paged you."

"I'm sorry—"

"Are you okay?"

"God, I'm so sorry, Alex. I must have lost track of time."

His gaze pierced through her, exposing her flimsy excuse for what it was, but he didn't ask any more questions. Instead, he walked over and rested his hand at her back, urging her toward the doors. "I'm happy you're okay. Now, tell me, where are we eating?"

Oh, no. She wanted to go home. "I'm not really hungry."

He stopped and stared at her intently, then said slowly, "Well, Miss Hannah, I'm starving." The tough glint in his eyes said he would take care of her, even if she wouldn't take care of herself. He was a bull rider, not a push over.

She sighed and told him about a place that had the best Mexican food this side of Texas. And, this time, she didn't step away from his touch as he walked her outside. She even leaned into him, just a little.

When they got on their way, she gave Alex directions and lay her head back, closing her eyes.

For once, he was quiet. He finally slowed and turned on his blinker.

She opened her eyes, and they were pulling into the small dirt parking lot of the little restaurant.

He smiled at her. "Better?"

"Yeah. Thanks." Somehow, this man always anticipated her needs.

As he opened his door, she opened hers. He stopped and turned to her. "Hannah, I'm taking you to dinner. Please allow me to help you out of the truck. It is what a gentleman does."

Her mouth dropped open, and she could only nod as heat rose up her neck. He wanted to treat her like a lady, and she didn't remember how to act like one anymore.

Alex opened her door and took her hand, gently helping her down from his tall truck. "I'll take care of you, Hannah, when you're with me. You deserve it." He looked into her eyes and held her gaze, urging her to believe in her worth.

Under his spell, she said slowly, "Thank you, Alex."

Hand at her back, he walked her inside the glass doors of the little restaurant.

When they were seated, rather than taking the chair across from her, he sat in the one next to her and smiled. "Tell me what is the best food here, Hannah."

"I love their carne guisada plate, but their fajita plate is amazing, too."

"I'll have the carne guisada." He folded his menu and laid it on the table. "And a beer."

Laying her menu down, she said, "I'll have the same thing, with iced tea." Having him so close set her nerves on edge. His cologne filled her nose, and it was so damn sexy. She knew it couldn't be real, but heat emanated from him, warming her from the inside. Imagining him slipping his arm around her sent tingles tickling their way up her belly. She could feel her face getting red and looked away from him.

"Hannah?"

Still looking away, she said, "Uh-huh?"

He took her hand from her lap and held it between his own. "Whatever is wrong, I'm here. You're safe with me. Okay?"

Closing her eyes, she took a deep breath. She hadn't fooled him or anyone else. Obviously, she was a wreck. She squeezed his hand. "Thanks." She couldn't quite look at him. Not yet. Instead she let her gaze travel over all the trinkets from Mexico hanging on the walls—beautiful sombreros, maracas, and little straw dolls. When her face felt its normal color, she turned back to him.

He gazed solemnly at her.

Their waitress came up just then, and they gave their orders.

Alex released her hand and cupped her face, caressing her cheek with his thumb before saying, "Chloe will love her new dresses. You give them to her. Monday, maybe you can help her try them on."

Hannah's heart leapt. Could this man read her mind? Smiling, she gripped his shoulder. "I'd like that. Thank you, Alex." She could almost feel the little girl in her arms right now. Pulse racing, she took several swallows of the iced tea the waitress set on the table.

Their dinners arrived a few minutes later, and Alex kept up a lively conversation, telling her about some of his near misses when he bucked off cantankerous bulls. Her appetite came back, and she demolished her carne guisada. It was hard to stay down around Alex. His up-beat personality could pull anyone out of the dumps.

Ever the gentleman, he helped her into the truck when they left the restaurant, setting her belly tingling again.

ALEX GLANCED AT HANNAH as he climbed into his truck. She had her head back, eyes closed, and her arm slung over the center console. The poor woman was exhausted, emotionally more than anything. What the hell had happened tonight? She'd scared him, disappearing like that. He'd even gone out to his truck. Something was terribly wrong. Hannah needed help.

He kept his speed down and eased to a stop at lights. Hannah must completely relax. It had turned dark while they were eating. When he left Carlsbad behind, only the glow from a half-moon and the stars illuminated the night. He picked up Hannah's hand and squeezed it gently. "Hannah?"

She looked at him muzzily. "Huh?"

"Can we talk?"

She blinked a couple of times. "About what?"

He squeezed her hand tighter. "What hurts you, Hannah? Tell me. Please." Holding her gaze, he did everything in his power to give her the courage to open her heart.

Raising her hand to his lips, he kissed her fingers.

Face slack, she stared at him, her eyes unfocused, as if she saw things he couldn't see.

Glancing back and forth between the road and her face, he waited for her to speak.

Finally, she said, "I can't have babies." Strained with pain, her voice broke, and she swallowed hard then stared out the windshield. "Ty and I tried for years." She told him about being tested, the cysts, and having them removed. "Even after my surgery, I still couldn't get pregnant, though the doctor expected I would." Her voice fractured, and she covered her mouth. "Ty blamed me. I think that's why he had the affair."

"¡*Fíofó*! What an asshole. If the man weren't dead, Alex would kill him. How could the man blame this sweet woman for something she couldn't help—for something that broke her heart? *Ay!* "This is not your fault, Hannah!"

In silence, her tears glistened in the starlight. Either she cried her heart out long ago, or she held her pain locked so far away she couldn't cry. It didn't matter. He couldn't sit here and let her suffer like this. He slowed and pulled off the road and into the grass, then turned the truck off.

Hannah didn't move.

He unhooked his seatbelt and lifted the console out of the way. Moving closer to her, he said, "Hannah, come to me. Let me hold you."

She reached up and wiped her cheeks, then eased toward him.

That was all he needed. He lifted her to his lap and wrapped his arms around her. Cuddling her as he would a small child, he kissed her temple and said, "*Meu querida, meu amor, você está seguro.*"

He rocked her, telling her she was safe, she was his sweetheart. He rocked her like he did Chloe when she woke with a bad dream. This woman had suffered terrible cruelty at the hands of her husband. Tightening his hold on her, he closed his eyes and prayed for healing for her injured mind and her broken heart.

As he expected, Hannah fell asleep. She'd relaxed into him like a child seeking solace. Examining her face, he realized how young she looked without the tense expression she always wore. She didn't seem at all like his rock-hard little boss. He raised her fingers to his lips and kissed them. Every protective instinct he had was screaming at him to take care of her. How could he help heal this hurt? It went so deep. Somehow, he would have to. Hannah couldn't go on living like this.

Though in an uncomfortable position, he closed his eyes and tried to relax. He wanted her to sleep at least an hour. She was completely limp in his arms, and her usually rock-hard muscles needed the break.

Hannah actually slept over two hours before she stirred. By then his legs felt nothing and his neck cramped. Why hadn't he gotten more comfortable before he put her in his lap? It was all worth it though, to feel her melt into him.

She opened her eyes appearing confused for a second or two. "Alex, thank you. I'm sorry I fell asleep." She struggled to get over into her seat.

He assisted her, then moved back behind the wheel. Before he started the truck, he caught and held her gaze. "Hannah, it was my privilege to hold you." She must understand that she shouldn't be embarrassed about tonight. Letting down her barriers had been hard for her. He wanted them to stay down. Wanted her to feel comfortable talking to him.

When he got back on the highway, he grinned at her. "Tomorrow, we will be tired. I'm glad it's Sunday."

She smiled back uneasily. "Me, too. I'm sleeping in."

He laughed. "You're lucky, Hannah. Chloe is a little girl who does not sleep in. I know that now."

"Why don't you bring her over tomorrow? I'll put her up on a horse. I know she'll love it. Stay for dinner. I'll make a casserole."

Her invitation sounded wonderful. He found himself thinking of Hannah constantly anyway. Weekends apart from her dragged for him. "Chloe will be a real cowgirl tomorrow." He reached for Hannah's hand, and she squeezed his fingers.

Later, he drove into her driveway and shut off the engine. After he helped her down from the truck, he picked up her hands and held her gaze. With gentle pressure, he eased her close and pulled her into a hug, resting his chin on her head. "Hannah, you're a good woman. You remember this." With his hand at her back, he walked her to her door. Somehow, he must help her find happiness. His time was limited, but with God, he could do it.

Chapter Seven

HANNAH'S HEART BEAT harder as Alex's truck pulled into the driveway Sunday afternoon. Anticipating his arrival had kept her on pins and needles. Despite knowing how it would end, she couldn't help wanting the man. She headed for the passenger side, where it was easier to reach Chloe in the back seat of the truck. She said, "Hey, Alex," when she opened the door, but her eyes stayed on the little girl.

"Hey, Hannah," and he stepped out.

Hannah pulled Chloe into her arms, kissing her, and met Alex as he rounded the truck. Damn, he had on a t-shirt again, leaving his gorgeous chest on display. No fair. "I saddled the horses. Are you two ready to ride?"

Chloe looked at Hannah.

She brushed wild curls from the little girl's face. "We're going to have fun today, sweetheart. Wait 'til you see."

Alex smiled. "We're ready."

"Okay, we'll take the Mule." The Kawasaki Mule, a small four-wheel-drive vehicle, was indispensable on the ranch.

When they got to the barn, she grabbed Chloe while Alex went inside and came back out leading her two horses.

She walked over. "Chloe, meet Rusty and Hershey. They're both sweet boys." Glancing at Alex, she said, "Do you want to carry Chloe, or shall I?"

He shrugged. "If the horse is gentle ..."

She set Chloe on the ground. "Hold right here, sweetie," and she gave the little girl a handhold on her shirt while she checked Rusty's cinch.

Alex did the same with Hershey. "These are quarter horses, Hannah?"

"Yes. These two are great at working cattle. Really quick on their feet."

Looking down, she gasped and reached for Rusty's back end. Chloe stood behind him, her tiny hand on his hock. As Hannah whisked the little girl away, Rusty flicked his tail, nothing more. Hannah shuddered. Hands shaking, she crouched down and clutched Chloe to her chest. "Honey, I told you to hold on to my shirt! Why did you let go? Never walk behind a horse. He could hurt you real bad. Do you hear me?"

Chloe began to cry.

Alex rushed over, leading Hershey. "What happened?"

Hannah, feeling lightheaded, even nauseated by the close call, told him, then said, "My God, Alex. She could have been killed." Her voice broke at the last, and she thrust Chloe at him. "I don't know what made me think I could ever be a mother!" Grabbing the reins of both horses, she headed for the barn.

Alex called, "Wait, Hannah!" and strode to the Mule, buckling Chloe safely in the seat.

He headed into the darkened barn and spied the horses tied to a pen. As he walked past them, he found Hannah, head pressed against Rusty's neck. "Hannah, it was not your fault. Children, they do these things. Believe me, Chloe, she is always getting into stuff. I can't take my eyes off her."

Without turning, Hannah said, "No, I shouldn't have put her down. I should have set her in the saddle or held her and let you check the cinch. That's what a real mother would have done. A real mother knows these things."

Alex stepped close and laid his hands on her shoulders, gently turning her toward him. "Hannah, real mothers are not always good mothers. A good mother wants to do the right thing, and that is you." He tilted her chin until her gaze met his. "You're good for my daughter, Hannah. I trust you. You must trust you, too." He pulled her closer and enveloped her in a warm hug, holding her there.

Stiff at first, unwilling to forgive herself, she eventually relaxed, unable to resist the warmth of his arms and the gentle way he held her.

He kissed her temple.

She turned her face to him, eyes closed, and sighed.

He kissed her cheek, and her jaw, and behind her ear.

She sucked in a breath.

He feathered a kiss across her lips.

She opened her eyes. Then closed them again.

Smiling, he captured her lips in a soft, gentle, lingering kiss. And stepped back.

When she opened her eyes again, he said, "Let's ride."

Emotions flooded her. What power did this man possess? The world had vanished while he held her in his arms. And her guilt, her anxiety, were gone. She licked her lips and nodded.

He untied the horses and led them out into the sunlight. She followed, changed by the man and his kiss and not sure what to do about it.

Once outside, she took the horses' reins while Alex unbuckled Chloe.

He said, "Hannah, Chloe rides with you."

She chewed her lip. He was obviously going with the old *if you fall off, get right back on the horse* thing. "Okay." Handing him Hershey's reins, she mounted Rusty. "Hand her up." She settled the little girl in front of her, and Chloe grabbed the saddle horn. "That's right. You hold on while we ride."

Alex mounted Hershey. "Ready, boss."

They moved away from the barn, passing the planted wheat fields, and emerging on one of the large desert pastures with uneven terrain where cattle grazed on sparse native grasses. Trees were sadly lacking in this arid West Texas land, but giant dagger yuccas dotted the landscape, along with barberry bushes and the sword-like lechegilla plants.

Rusty jerked his head as a roadrunner sped across the road several feet in front of the horses. Hannah glanced at Chloe, who had been mostly silent, her big blue eyes taking in everything around her. "Are you having fun, honey?"

She nodded her head and grinned.

"Did you see that bird run across the road? That's called a roadrunner. It hardly flies at all. It runs real fast everywhere it goes."

Chloe said, "Woawunnah."

Hannah laughed and squeezed her, adoring her little voice. "That's a hard one to say, isn't it?" Hannah loved being horseback if it didn't involve cattle, and this ride, with the precious child in front of her, was magical. Pointing to the base of a smaller, soaptree yucca, she said, "Chloe, look at the green lizard." The Texas collared lizard, with its bright blue-green color and distinctive black collar around its throat, was a beautiful creature. She stopped the horse so Chloe could take a good look. "Isn't it pretty?"

Chloe stared, her mouth slightly open. "Pwetty."

Alex said, "That is my first. Do you have many here?"

Thus far during the ride, she'd kept her gaze strictly ahead and away from the gorgeous cowboy. Now tingles of attraction tickled her. His kiss had awakened something in her, and she found herself wanting more of that closeness despite her knowledge that he would be out of her life soon. "I don't know. I don't see them that often."

Chloe had begun to babble. Some words Hannah could understand, and others she couldn't. The little girl reached down and clutched a handful of Rusty's mane, yanking on it, though the horse didn't seem to mind. She looked up and pointed at a butterfly that floated in front of Rusty's head. "Pwetty."

Hannah kissed her cheek, cherishing the moment, wanting this ride to last forever. "That's a butterfly, Chloe. He is pretty."

Alex nudged Hershey closer and squeezed Hannah's knee. "Chloe is having fun, Hannah." He smiled at her, the light in his eyes melting her resolve to keep her distance.

She said, "I love riding out here. Some people think the desert's ugly, but I couldn't disagree more. There's so much life, and the wildflowers in spring and summer give it such color. It's peaceful. I can think when I'm out here alone."

He nodded, searching her face. "That is good, Hannah."

Casting her gaze around them, she pulled Rusty to a stop. "We should probably get back. This little one will be hungry by the time we're home."

"Would you like me to hold her now?" Alex asked.

Her arms tightened. "No. She's no trouble."

Soon, Chloe's head sank onto Hannah's arm. She slept, rocked by the rhythm of Rusty's stride.

Hannah held her close, protective and oh-so-joyful at having the tiny bundle in her arms. Rusty needed no guidance. He knew they were headed home.

Alex appeared lost in thought.

Silence settled on them. The only sound the plop, plop, plop of the horses' shod hooves on the dirt road and the occasional clack as one of them kicked a stone.

When they arrived at the barn, she motioned for Alex to take Chloe. Hannah made short work of unsaddling and turning out the horses.

The little girl woke when Hannah started the Mule. Looking up from her father's chest, Chloe stretched her arms out for Hannah.

A surge of emotion slammed Hannah's heart as she reached for Chloe. Never had Hannah felt this connection, this wanting, this need for a child. As Hannah pulled Chloe into a warm embrace, she snuggled into her, wrapping her arms around Hannah's neck. Overcome, she closed her eyes, caressing Chloe's long, tight curls, inhaling her childlike fragrance, knowing she could never let this child go.

Alex said, "Do you want me to drive?"

Eyes closed, she nodded and scooted over.

On the way home, she stared, unseeing into the distance.

Once at the house, she fixed Chloe, who was now wide awake, a snack.

Alex sat next to Hannah at the table and touched her arm. "Thank you for today. We had fun."

His smile, which always lit his beautiful brown eyes with warmth, eased Hannah's heart, and she felt more herself.

"I enjoyed taking the afternoon off, and I can't remember the last time I went riding for fun." She couldn't help it. Her eyes strayed to his muscular chest, his strong shoulders and back to that beautiful smile. Her body responded with a quickening pulse and butterflies in her tummy. She wet her lips.

Alex grinned and clasped her hand. "Hannah, I want to take you on a real date."

She sucked in a breath, needing to say *no*, but wanting to say *yes*.

"Come on, Hannah. We will eat, and dance, and have fun, okay?"

Chloe knocked her milk over and cried.

Hannah jumped up. "It's okay, honey. You didn't mean to. I'll clean it up." Grabbing some paper towels, Hannah had the spill wiped away quickly.

Chloe stopped crying as soon as she saw Hannah wasn't mad.

Did Debra scold the child for mistakes? Anger caused a hot burning sensation in Hannah's stomach. How dare that woman? Every child had accidents. They shouldn't get punished for them.

Hannah took a deep breath. Her emotions were all over the map today. Way too strong. Maybe she needed to go out and blow off steam. She glanced at Alex as she sat back down and her tummy fluttered again. She wanted to be with this handsome cowboy, and she couldn't deny herself any longer. "Alex, I'd love to go on a real date with you. Just tell me when."

He grinned. "Next Saturday night," and reached for her hand. "Hannah, thank you."

A little while later, before Alex loaded Chloe into her car seat, he said, "Say goodbye to Hannah, Chloe."

Steeling herself for the sweep of intense emotion as Chloe held out her little hands, Hannah took the child in her arms and gave her a hug and kiss.

Chloe said, "Bye, bye."

A lump in her throat, Hannah nodded. "Bye, honey." As she watched the two of them drive off a few minutes later, her heart followed them. She longed for the little girl already, and it would only get worse over the next couple of days. And there was something else. A part of her ached for the handsome cowboy and his tender hands, too.

Chapter Eight

THE FOLLOWING SATURDAY night, Alex handed the menu to the waitress after ordering his steak. Hannah had already ordered and drank a margarita while he sipped a beer. Since he was driving, he would drink very little.

Hannah looked lovely. Her black blouse set off her copper hair and blue eyes and he'd never realized how sexy freckles could be. His fingers itched to open the buttons of her top and see how far the little golden speckles went. He swept his gaze across the nearly empty restaurant before she could guess his thoughts.

"How did you learn to speak English so well, Alex?"

Her smile and the interest in her eyes sent tingles across his chest. How lucky he was to have the company of this woman tonight. "I studied English for three years in my off seasons. The PBR encouraged me. They want us Brazilians to talk good on TV." He laughed. "I worked hard. I didn't like talking with the interpreter. It was too slow." Taking a swallow of beer, he said, "Anyway, I wanted to live in the U.S., so talking English was important. I still must learn more. Many words, I don't understand. I carry a dictionary with me."

She grinned. "Really?"

"Oh, sure. I find words all the time. Spelling the words, now, that is hard. I ask people how to spell a lot."

She took a drink of her iced tea. "I admire you, Alex. I know some Spanish because I took it in school. But becoming fluent and speaking it every day—I've never been able to do that."

Tonight, he enjoyed watching Hannah's eyes as she talked. Different colors of blue shaded them, and they sparkled, something they rarely did while she worked on the ranch. He hadn't been this attracted to a woman since his divorce. The sound of her voice was enough to send his pulse racing. "Some Brazilian cowboys don't try too hard to speak English. English is not easy, you know?" He smiled as the light created golden highlights in her hair.

"It isn't, is it?" Hannah took a sip of tea. "Alex, I hope you don't mind me asking, but have you heard from Chloe's mother?"

He shook his head. "No. But this does not surprise me. She calls me only when she wants money."

"Oh."

They continued their easy conversation until dinner was over, and he handed his card to the waitress. "Are you ready to dance, Hannah?"

She blushed. "I haven't been dancing in a long time. I may step all over your toes."

"I might step on your toes, too. It's good we both have boots."

She fiddled with her napkin. "Just don't laugh if I trip or something."

He reached for her hand. "Hannah, I'll hold you. We will be the best dancers on the dance floor tonight."

She cracked up. "Uh, right."

They finished their meal and, after signing the ticket, he helped Hannah with her chair and escorted her to his truck. Funny thing, he wasn't even six feet tall, but he always felt huge when he walked with the tiny woman.

A short time later, they pulled into the parking lot of the club. As he escorted her to the front doors, he imagined what it would feel like to two-step around the dance floor, holding Hannah close to his body as she swayed to the music. He felt focused again after two years of treading water, like a swimmer lost at sea. This woman was the reason. Placing his hand at Hannah's back, he urged her through the doors.

The place was a little small, but the dance floor was large enough for a fair number of couples. The dim light, except near the bars, made it a cozy setting. The band arrived on stage for another set. He found a table and seated Hannah then left to get their drinks. The first song had begun when he sat opposite her. "This is nice, huh?"

She fidgeted and had a hard time meeting his gaze as she took a big gulp of her drink. "Yeah, real nice."

He reached over and took her hand, holding it gently in his fingers. "Hannah, it is just you and me. Relax. We have all night. No rush."

Nodding, she seeming more at ease. "Okay, Alex. Thanks. You know, Ty was so ... and before, we were so stressed out. It's just been a long time for, for all this—and being with another man." She shook her head and turned away.

Even in the dim light he could see the deep red creeping up her face. He got up and moved his chair beside her. Slipping his arm around her, he kissed her temple. "*Meu querida*, the past does not matter to us." He tipped her chin so she looked into his eyes. "*Relaxa, meu querida.*" He kissed her. "Now we have fun, sweetheart."

They watched the dancers circle the dance floor, and she slowly relaxed into him. He kissed her temple again. Hannah was safe with him. More than anything else, she was protected from her own fears.

Soon he signaled the waitress for another round. It would be his last beer, but Hannah needed to unwind. The bourbon would release her inhibitions and allow her to enjoy herself tonight. With her snuggled close against his chest, he pointed out couples who were good dancers, speaking into her ear to be heard over the loud music coming from the stage. Her hair tickled him, and his desire quickened, though he tried hard to tamp it down. Right now, Hannah needed him to be calm.

After her second drink, he caught Hannah's boot tapping to the music. When the next slow song started, he stood. "Dance with me please, Hannah?"

She stared at him with startled eyes, then got up. "Thank you."

His hand at her back, he escorted her to the dance floor, anticipating holding her slim body.

Taking her in his arms, he stood still for a moment to let her get her balance, then stepped out with the slow beat of the music. Her stiff body told him how nervous she was. He guided her with a firm hand at her waist and clear signals in the palm of her hand, preparing her for each step he made. Soon her body unwound, and he pulled her close. She melted into him, and they moved as one to the music. With Hannah curled on his chest, moving against his hips, his pulse pounded in his ears, and he tightened his arm around her. Taking a deep breath, he mentally talked himself down. Too soon, the song ended, and he released her.

She stepped back, and her half-lidded eyes reflected some of his own desire.

He kept hold of her hand. "Thank you, Hannah."

"You're a good dancer, Alex. We didn't step on each other once."

Laughing, he put his arm around her, leading her off the dance floor. "I told you I wouldn't let you trip."

When they took their seats, Hannah flipped her hair off her shoulder and grinned at him. It was the first time he'd seen her truly happy, and she was magnificent. He wrapped her in a hug. "Hannah, you should be happy all the time."

Still in his embrace, she clung to him. "Alex, I *am* happy tonight. Thank you." Her eyes closed, and she smiled. It melted his heart.

He squeezed her for a moment, then turned her loose. He would do his best to see she stayed that way.

A few minutes later, a fast song started, and he said, "Are you ready to dance, Hannah?"

She raised her brows, looking unsure. "You have my back, right?"

He laughed. "I have your back. Come."

Once on the dance floor, he waited again to be sure she was ready, then stepped out, dancing to the rapid beat of the song. To his surprise, Hannah was right with him. He spun, and she kept up with him. Soon they were twirling and quick-stepping all over the dance floor. When the music stopped, they were both breathing fast. "Hannah, you teased me. You're a very good dancer."

"We both are. That was fun, Alex."

He settled her at the table and excused himself. "I'll be back. Would you like another drink?"

"One more. Thank you, Alex."

HANNAH'S GAZE FOLLOWED Alex as he wove his way through the tables to the restrooms, the vision of his sexy back side doing nothing to calm the tingling in every nerve in her body. The protective way he held her, his gentle kisses, his sweet smile, everything about him tonight turned her on. Deep in her core, lust snaked and coiled, ready to be released. How long had it been since she felt this way? For years, she and Ty had been going through the motions, watching her temp and hoping for a pregnancy. Romance had been the casualty of their dreams for a child. This night was magical, her body more alive with every breath she took. Alex would leave her, she knew that, but tonight it didn't matter. Tonight, he belonged to her.

Alex returned to the table, setting her glass in front of her and sliding his arm around her as if it had always belonged there. "Hannah, I'm happy." He tilted his head so she could look into his eyes. "You make me happy, Hannah."

She sucked in her bottom lip. To hell with the consequences. "You make me happy, too, Alex."

Leaning in, he swept her lips with a kiss. Then kissed her again, lingering over it.

Her heart pounded, and she reached up, capturing his cheek with her palm. When he pulled back, she looked into his eyes and grinned. "Your kisses make me happy, Alex."

He threw his head back and laughed. "Hannah, *meu querida*, I like your kisses too."

She finished her drink, cuddled in his arms, happiness humming in her veins. When he asked her to dance again, the music was slow, and she settled into his body like she was born there. He held her close, and, as the music stopped, he leaned down and kissed her. Her heart swelled with such joy she wanted to cry.

As they arrived at the table, he said, "Are you ready to leave?"

The look in his eyes said he wanted more than holding her on the dance floor. Her stomach clenched. Was she ready for that? This had been an amazing evening, and she didn't want it to stop. But, how much farther would she go? He was leaving. She couldn't forget that. Nodding, she said, "It's a long way home. Let's go."

He held her hand in the truck, keeping up a lazy conversation.

She asked, "Do you have any brothers or sisters?"

A look of sadness flitted across his face. "No. My mother was a kitchen maid on a big *rancho*. I don't know my father. She came there when she was pregnant with me. It was always me and my *maē*. She never talked about her family. I don't know if she didn't have one, or if they didn't want her when she got pregnant."

Hannah squeezed his hand. "I'm sorry, Alex. That must have been hard for both of you."

"The *rancho* where I grew up was very grand, very beautiful. And the people were good to me and my mother. That is where I learned to ride bulls." He grinned at her. "Come closer, Hannah." Flipping the console up, he jerked the seat belt out. "You will be safe here beside me."

He had the devil in his eyes, and her body responded. Yanking her belt off, she slid next to him, but, before she belted in, she pulled his face to her and kissed him, hard.

When she leaned back, he grinned. "You kiss good, Hannah."

Buckling up, her heart beat a million times a minute. She wanted her hands all over that muscular chest of his. Wanted to be on her knees beside him, kissing his sensuous mouth, exploring every inch of him. She hardly knew herself at the moment, and didn't care one bit.

Alex clasped her leg and pulled her closer to him, smiling down at her.

She leaned into him, and he slid his arm around her shoulders. Snuggling into his chest, she closed her eyes, reveling in the sensations her body was feeling. Nerves sang everywhere he touched her.

He said, "Hannah."

"Hmm?"

"Kiss me again."

She smiled and did what she wanted to do—unbuckled and rose to her knees, taking his face in her hands.

Looking at her, smiling, he waited for her to do what she willed with him. He glanced at the road, then back at her.

Caressing his lips with hers, she tickled him with the tip of her tongue, and dipped inside.

Groaning, he whispered, "Hannah." Looking quickly at the road, he returned to her.

She kissed him again and sat back on her heels.

He licked his lips, shaking his head. "Damn. I want to kiss you back."

"You asked for it."

Keeping his eyes on the road, he grinned. "I sure did."

She sat down and buckled in, leaning into him as he put his arm around her again.

He kissed the top of her head, and hugged her against him. "Hannah, I want you." Then he kissed her again. "But I worry. You need a man who will be here with you, work your ranch and take care of you all the time. A bull rider is gone too much. I could not be that man for you."

She didn't want to hear his words. Couldn't think that far ahead tonight. Nodding, she said, "I know. I've thought about that, too." Her body wanted him. Her heart yearned for him. Nothing could stop those two things from happening tonight.

Squeezing her again, he said, "I don't want to hurt you, Hannah. You hurt too bad already."

Dammit, it had been so long. She *would* have this one night of happiness. Fortunately, there were a few advantages to being tiny. Throwing off her seatbelt, she swung astride Alex, and looked him in the eyes. "I don't want to remember yesterday, and I don't want to think about tomorrow. I want to be happy tonight. Will you make me happy, Alex?"

He glanced at the road and then back at her. "*Meu queridinho*. I will, my little sweetheart."

She smiled and kissed him, slipping her tongue inside and stroking him. "You drive. I'll kiss."

"*Santa mãe de Deus.*" He groaned. "Holy mother of God, Hannah!"

She slipped the tip of her tongue in his ear and puffed a tiny breath.

He ducked and moaned, "Hannah, I'll wreck." Yet, he caught her mouth and kissed her hard.

Evidence of his extreme arousal was underneath her. Tilting her head so he could see the road, she kissed him with tiny, feathery kisses, exploring every bit of his mouth. Sliding her lips down, she nibbled on his neck.

Sucking in a hard breath, his hand on her back clenched.

Smiling. she kissed him some more, making her way to the hollow of his throat. With quick fingers, she unbuttoned his shirt.

He sucked in his belly, hissing, "Hannah, you're killing me!"

Sliding her hands inside his shirt, she ran her fingers over the delicious muscles of his chest. She caught his mouth in hers and kissed him deeply. "Alex, you're gorgeous."

Groaning he said sharply, "Hannah, I'm pulling over if you don't stop."

She grinned. "Against the rules. You drive. I kiss, remember?"

He narrowed his eyes at her. "We will be home soon, Hannah. I will have revenge."

A trickle of delicious fear swirled in her belly. What kind of actions would this gorgeous man take with her? She held his face in her hands again, and kissed him, taking her time, enjoying every second. If this was the only night she had, she would make it count.

Later, as they pulled into her driveway, Alex gave her a mischievous grin. He got out as she slid over to her side, wondering what he had planned for her.

The door beside her flew open, and Alex lifted her out, holding her against the side of the truck, eye-level with him. "You will invite me in, Hannah."

She swallowed, trying not to smile. "Won't you come inside, Alex?"

He set her on the ground, reached into the glovebox for something, and grabbed her purse from the floorboard. Grinning, he said, "I will, Hannah."

He slung his arm around her shoulders as they walked to the door.

Once she locked the door behind them, he lifted her into his arms and carried her into the kitchen, sitting her on the countertop, facing him. "Do you have anything to drink, Hannah?"

She bit her lip, holding back a smile. "Um, bourbon?"

"I'll get it." He located the bottle by the sink, found two glasses and poured three fingers in each glass. Handing her one, he narrowed his eyes and said, "This is for your courage, Hannah."

Her eyes widened. She took too big a swallow, then choked, coughing and spitting bourbon everywhere.

Alex laughed and grabbed her glass, patting her on the back. "Come on, Hannah. You're a tough boss lady. What are you afraid of, eh?"

Her eyes watering, she took a good look at him. He was grinning, his eyes loaded with mischief. Lord, what had she gotten herself into?

He handed her the glass back. "Drink up. You will need it."

She chugged the bourbon like water, hoping to fortify herself for whatever this Brazilian devil had in store for her.

Slapping her back, he said, "That's my girl," and downed his own drink. Sliding her off the counter, he clasped her butt in his large hands, holding her to his waist.

She wrapped her legs around him. Pulse racing, heart pounding, surges of desire sweeping through her, she was his.

He kissed her and whispered in her ear. "Tell me where to go, *meu amor*."

Giving him directions, she lay her head on his chest, enjoying the magic of the moment, the wonder of his arms, the anticipation of loving him.

Dropping his hat on the dresser, he set her on the bed and knelt in front of her. When he put his fingers to the first button of her blouse, he said, "Finally, an answer to my question."

His gentle touch sent chills of desire racing through her. Her bra suddenly felt too tight. She furrowed her brow. What question?

As he loosened several more buttons, he said, "Ah, there."

"What?"

"Your spots end here."

"Oh." She didn't like her freckles and felt herself blushing.

He took her face in his hands. "Oh, no, Hannah. Your spots make you beautiful. Your skin is like the sun. I don't know the word. Like when the sun shines. *Brilhante*.

His lips sought hers in a gentle kiss as he finished unbuttoning her blouse. He pulled back and gazed into her eyes. "I want to make love to you, Hannah."

She ran her thumb across his lip. "Alex, I want you. I don't know what I'll do after tonight, or how I'll feel. But, right now I don't care. I want to love you all night long."

He grinned. "Hannah, I can do that." Slipping her blouse off her shoulders, he pulled her to her feet.

She forced herself to be brave. It had been a long time since a man other than Ty had looked at her.

He slid his arms around her and unhooked her bra, dropping it on the bed. Stepping back, he looked at her.

His gaze tickled her as if it were his fingers. She shivered.

His voice husky, he said, "Hannah, you're beautiful."

His words reassured her. She reached for her belt buckle.

He stopped her. "It is my pleasure to undress you tonight."

She stood still as he unhooked her belt and unfastened her Wranglers. Desire awakened in her core as she watched his every move. When he slid her jeans down her legs, his breath puffed on her bare belly. The thrill was so intense, she trembled. He eased her down on the edge of the bed and removed her boots and socks. He kissed her toes, and she giggled breathlessly. Slipping her jeans off, he lifted her to her feet.

Pulling her hair forward so the copper waves spilled down her chest, he said, "Hannah, you must believe me. You're perfect."

She smiled. His sweet words filled her with joy, and her fingers twitched with the need to touch him.

He yanked down the bedspread and sheet and reached for her.

She stopped him. "Your turn, but you can help me. I'm in a hurry." Grinning. she grabbed the first button of his shirt.

He laughed and unhooked his belt and unbuttoned his Wranglers. Using his toe, he pulled first one boot off, then the other. Unabashed, he removed his briefs with his jeans.

As she slid his shirt off his shoulders, he stood naked before her, grinning and ready to take her to bed. She couldn't help it, she laughed at his sheer self-confidence. "You bull riders. You're something else."

He launched himself into the bed, pulling her with him. They landed with a bounce, and she kept on laughing. Meeting her gaze, he settled her on top of him, wrapping his arms around her waist.

She raised herself on her forearms. "You've been really good to me, Alex. I'm so thankful Todd introduced us."

Alex sat up and kissed her, smiling. "I'm the one who is thankful, Hannah. I didn't know I was unhappy until I met you."

His words went straight to her heart. It was similar to how she felt. Fear slammed into her when she thought of him leaving, and she ruthlessly pushed it out of her mind. She had tonight to love him. "Alex," she caressed him with her lips, "you make me happy, too."

She reached to turn off the lamp, and he touched her arm. "Can we leave it on, Hannah?"

Dammit, she felt herself blushing again. "Okay."

He said, "I got a condom out of my truck."

Intense sadness slammed her. She closed her eyes. "I can't get pregnant, remember?"

He pulled her down and kissed her. "I wanted you to be sure. And, I'm healthy. I got checked."

She sighed, looking at him. "Likewise. I did that first thing after I found out about Ty's affair."

Smiling, he rolled her on her back, leaning above her. "Someone got a little crazy tonight. Am I correct?" He clasped her wrists and raised them over her head. "I think her name is Hannah."

She giggled, her heart pounding. Here it was. His revenge for her outlandish behavior on the way home. She tried to pull her hands down, but it was useless.

He grinned. "No, no, my little one, it is my turn now." He kneed her legs apart and rested on her, lowering his lips to hers.

She expected a deep, sensual payback kiss, but was disappointed. Tiny butterfly kisses teased her mouth, and she pressed forward, wanting more.

He retreated. The tip of his tongue traced the seam of her lips, but when she opened her mouth to accept him, it was gone. She moaned, then begged, "Alex, kiss me."

Laughing, he nibbled her neck, still holding her arms helplessly above her head. "*Meu amor, você vai pagar*."

Exasperated, she said, "If you're going to torture me, at least speak English."

He laughed. "I'm sorry. I'll make you pay, my love. That is all I said."

Her eyes grew round as he studied a cylindrical pillow tied generously with red ribbon that lay beside the bed.

Grinning, he lunged for it, untying the two ribbons and coming back to her. "I have a good idea, Miss Hannah. I'll tie you up. I say it is fair."

She groaned. Alex didn't scare her, but damn, the things he could do to her. He was right, though, it was only fair. She had had her way with him while he was stuck driving the truck. "Go ahead."

"Yes! Thank you, Hannah." Using the ribbons, he tied each wrist to a rung of the headboard, leaving the loop plenty loose.

"I can untie this if you want me to. Don't worry." He leaned in and kissed her, caressing her tongue with his.

What she wanted most was his hands on her body, his mouth on hers, him making love to her, now.

He sat back on his knees and eyed her, smiling. "Oh, you're in trouble now, Hannah." He reached up and cupped her face. "If you want me to untie you, ask me. I will do it."

She looked into his eyes and trusted him.

ALEX STOOD AND PUSHED the covers off the foot of the bed, then lay down next to Hannah, his head propped on his arm. He met her gaze, trailing his finger from the hollow of her throat, between her breasts, to her sweet patch of curly copper hair. He breathed deeply. Having her beside him, beautiful and vulnerable, made him want to love her all night long, just as she had requested. If he didn't get himself under control, however, that wouldn't happen. He trailed his fingertip down her midline again.

She shivered and closed her eyes.

He drew circles around her nipple, and she pulled in a breath, eyes still closed. Leaning down, he took the round pebble into his mouth and sucked hard. A spurt of desire shocked him. Damn!

Hannah arched up and moaned.

Mentally shaking himself, he slid his palm in slow circles on her tummy, continuing to suckle but gently now.

Her hip tipped up, and she bent her knee. "Alex?"

"Yes, my love?"

She moaned again.

Moving to the other breast, he teased her nipple, suckling softly. Cupping her mound, he slipped his finger inside and found her sensitive spot. It was warm and hard.

She sucked in a breath. "Alex!"

He rose up and kissed her. Though he wanted to tease her, he was having a terrible time controlling his own body. Rock hard now, every time he touched her his pulse sped faster.

Capturing his lips, she pressed into him, wanting more.

He pulled back. "Not so fast, *meu amor*, we have all night." Or, he hoped they did. This gorgeous woman was driving him to the edge.

Groaning, she pleaded, "Alex. Kiss me!"

He laughed and tickled her mouth with the tip of his tongue.

She moaned. "I'm sorry for the way I teased you. Kiss me, please."

He rewarded her begging. As he kissed her, his feelings for her grew stronger. How could he care so much for Hannah when they'd known each other only two months? Yet, he did care, deeply. When he said *meu amor*, that's what he felt—that he loved her. He knew it couldn't be true, it was too soon, but it felt so real. What started out as a tender kiss became much more. Exploring her lips, he delved deep, twining his tongue with hers.

Slipping his finger inside her, he matched his thrusts with his kisses.

Hannah moaned his name, kissing him back, panting and pushing up with her hips.

Her response so aroused him, he had to pull back.

She cried, "Alex!" and moaned again, her voice trailing into a sob.

She didn't say *untie me*. "I'm here." He slid to the bottom of the bed, between her legs, cradling her butt in his hands. He found her sensitive spot with the tip of his tongue.

Hannah called out his name, her voice shaking, arching her hips into him.

He circled the spot, caressed it, teased it with his tongue as she trembled, wanting more. Delving inside her, she shuddered. He worked his magic, bringing her to the brink of ecstasy—then he stood and lay by her side again.

Hannah, trembling all over, pulled at her bonds. "Alex, Alex, now. I need you. Stop this. Make love to me."

Still, she didn't say the words. But he couldn't take that tremble in her voice. He leaned in and kissed her, while untying one hand, then the other.

As soon as she was released, she dragged his face to her and kissed him hard, then grabbed his cock in her hand. A shudder ran through him. His heart pounded against his breast bone. He sucked in a breath and said, "Hannah, no, I'll—"

She slid down in the bed and settled her warm lips on him.

He clasped her head in his hands. Ripples of intense pleasure spread through him as she sucked him, root to tip. He couldn't stop her now. He didn't have the will. Her tongue slithered around him, and he gasped. His breath came in pants as Hannah pleasured him. It had been such a long, long time since making love had been this good. Finally, he could take no more, and he pulled her up. "Stop, Hannah, or I'll come."

He tilted her face so she looked at him. "How do you like to make love, Hannah? What is your favorite way?"

She didn't answer, holding herself very still.

"*Meu querida*, this is natural. I want to please you."

Biting her lip, she whispered. "Um, doggie style?"

He laughed. "Oh, ho, that is a favorite of mine, too." He got to his knees and settled her in front of him. "Now, *meu cão menina*, we will make love, my little doggie." The sight of her little ass, spread before him, almost caused him to lose control.

She glanced back at him.

Shit, she was sexy. *Meu deus*. Maybe he did love her. Knowing it had been a long time since she'd been with a man, he eased inside her.

She pushed into him and moaned softly.

He closed his eyes. He had to make this perfect for her. He entered her a little faster the second time, but still gently. Each stroke, he increased his pace, and soon Hannah rose to meet him. She had the rhythm. Chills ran through him. They were made for each other. Closing his eyes, he pumped into her, each glorious thrust taking him closer and closer to ecstasy.

Hannah shrieked his name.

That was all it took. With a final stroke, he spilled into her, clutching her hips against him. Her spasms milked him, continuing his pleasure.

She said, "Oh, Alex," and lay down on the bed.

He curled around her in a fuzzy cloud of spent desire. Running his hand up and down her arm, he whispered in her ear, "Hannah, that was beautiful."

She sniffed.

Alarmed, he said, "Hannah?" and reached for her face.

She caught his hand just as a tear touched his fingertip. "You're right. It was beautiful. Thank you for loving me."

He snugged her as close to him as possible and kissed the top of her head. "Hannah, you're very welcome. This is one of the best nights of my life."

She sucked in a ragged breath. "Me, too."

Hannah—had he hurt her? He only wanted to love her. He said, "You want to make love all night, am I right?"

"Maybe I overestimated myself."

He brought her fingers to his lips. "We will see about that, Hannah."

Chapter Nine

THE FOLLOWING MORNING, Hannah set a wall between them. After telling Alex she was going down to feed, she offered him coffee then asked him to lock up when he left. Surprised, he asked her if she was okay. She smiled and said, "I'm fine. Just busy," and walked out the door.

Two weeks later, Alex woke early with Hannah on his mind. As always. Things had been strained with her since the night they made love. He didn't understand. Making love to Hannah had meant so much to him. Changed him, even. He hadn't pursued the subject, though. He told her the truth that night they drove home. Hannah needed a different kind of man. Yet working with her and having such distance between them was killing him. He wanted to take her in his arms, kiss her lips, and make her uncaring look go away.

He'd planted the hay weeks ago. Now, when Hannah didn't send him elsewhere, they worked side-by-side mending fence. She didn't speak to him unless their work required it, and replied with few words if he spoke to her. It hurt, but maybe this meant she was protecting herself because he was leaving soon.

Now that he and Hannah were working on the fences and unable to care for a small child safely, Becky had found a woman in Barbwire to watch Chloe during the day. He'd expected Hannah to be upset, but all she did was bite that beautiful lip of hers and nod when he told her.

His head said this gulf between them was better. When he left, Hannah wouldn't suffer. But his heart cried *no!* It wanted his *querida,* needed to love her—wanted her in his bed, in his arms, in his life forever.

He rolled out of bed and slid on some sweatpants, heading into Todd's exercise room. Alex had been working out since his arrival months ago, but his injuries weren't mending the way he knew they should. He remembered how his first broken pelvis felt as it healed, and this pelvic injury was nothing like it. The pain was so excruciating that he still couldn't add weight while he worked his quadriceps and hamstrings.

And his weak riding arm couldn't lift much weight, even with the brace Dr. Freeman had reluctantly given him. His arm didn't actually grab, but it didn't move quite right, either.

When he'd been injured, the bull first knocked heads with Alex, rendering him unconscious, and then it lost its footing and rolled on him, breaking his pelvis and two ribs. Despite the efforts of three bullfighters, the bull went at Alex with his horns, lifting his limp body into the air and slinging him to the ground, crushing his riding arm. It broke in so many places, when Alex viewed the X-ray, he nearly vomited.

His fears grew daily. Despite how hard he worked in the gym, his injuries weren't healing. Dr. Freeman may have been right. His riding career might be over. A stab of panic left him breathless. He'd always thought there would be years to plan his retirement. But his body couldn't lie.

He threw himself down on the weight bench. Clearing his mind of doubt, he began his routine. He *would* ride again.

HANNAH TIGHTENED HER hold on the pliers, kinking the wire, then adding more kinks every couple of inches. Testing the now-taut strand with two fingers, she moved down to the next one. She glanced at Alex who stood down the fence line several feet. He squatted, mending the wire below hers. Something had plowed through the fence, breaking the bottom wires. Probably a damn javelina.

Working next to Alex was miserable. She tried to distance herself from her feelings for him. Her memory of his tenderness and her joy in their love making was too overwhelming, though. As much as she tried to focus on him leaving, she could only think of him loving her. What was wrong with her? Didn't she have any sense of self-preservation?

Alex had been right to find someone else to care for Chloe. It was okay to keep her when the little girl could stay in the truck with Hannah much of the day, but mending fence was long, grueling work. Still, she missed Chloe terribly. Her arms ached to hold her. Hannah dreamed of the texture of Chloe's skin, the sweet scent at the crease of her neck, and of running her fingers through Chloe's soft, tight curls.

The dark circles under Hannah's eyes, which had almost disappeared, were back with a vengeance. She tossed and turned at night, missing Alex, missing Chloe, and miserable at the thought of losing them both. It was like her past, when Ty loved another woman and ignored her plea to work on their marriage. There was nothing she could do to prevent Alex from leaving her—and taking Chloe with him. She sighed deeply.

Alex glanced up with a question in his eyes.

"About time for lunch." She headed for the truck.

They sat side-by-side in silence for a few minutes, then Alex said, "Chloe wants you, Hannah. She keeps asking."

Hannah squeezed her eyes shut. "I miss her, too." Agony filled her chest. The poor little thing didn't understand. She only knew her life had abruptly changed again. Hannah spit her bite of sandwich into a napkin, suddenly feeling like she might throw up. Stuffing the rest of her lunch into a bag, she shoved her door open and strode to the back of the truck. *This sucked! Why did life have to be so damn awful?*

Alex came around to the back, his arms folded and staring out into the distance. "Hannah, I'm sorry. You hurt, and I never wanted that." He reached for her hand but she pulled it away. "You're right to protect yourself from me. I understand. But can you see Chloe? You can come to Todd's, if it's easier."

This was all too much. She wanted to throw herself at him, feel him squeeze her tight, forget that he was leaving. She bit her lip, hard. He was right. She had to see Chloe. "Bring her here, Alex. Tomorrow's Saturday. About three? I'd love to see her." Yanking her leather gloves off, she said, "Let's knock off early today. Mending fence is a pain in the ass."

Alex laughed and headed over to pick up their tools.

She climbed into the truck and closed her eyes, wondering how her heart would bear it when she held the little girl in her arms again.

SATURDAY AFTERNOON, Hannah slid a pot of beans off the burner to cool and spread butter on top of the cornbread.

Alex and Chloe were due any minute, and Hannah couldn't stand still.

Chloe was all Hannah had been able to think about since deciding to see the child again. A truck pulled into the driveway, and Hannah looked out the living room window. Her heart leapt when Alex stepped out. What would she do when he drove away in that truck for the last time? Shuddering, she closed her eyes, unable to bear the thought.

As Alex approached the house with Chloe in his arms, Hannah's avid gaze absorbed every detail of the little girl's appearance. Had she grown? She looked pale, didn't she? Was she eating right? Who was this woman taking care of Chloe, anyway? Rushing to the door, Hannah threw it open before Alex could knock. "Hi, come in," she said, breathlessly.

He grinned and stepped inside. "Hello, Hannah."

Chloe leaned toward her, arms outstretched. "Hama."

Hannah's heart leapt as she pulled Chloe close. It was the first time she'd heard Chloe try to say her name. "When did she start saying that?"

Alex laughed. "I told you, she missed you. That is when."

Hannah kissed her cheek, and cuddled Chloe into her neck. "You're my smart girl, aren't you?" *God, how I've missed this. I can't let her go.*

Hannah carried the little girl into the kitchen, giving herself time to control her emotions. Chloe was leaving, and there was nothing Hannah could do about it. "Would you like a cookie? Just a little one, because we're having dinner soon."

Chloe nodded, smiling all the way up to her big blue eyes.

Alex had followed them to the kitchen, and he stood beside Hannah.

Despite her wishes, tiny fingers of craving crawled up her belly. She sighed, giving up. This special, gorgeous man would always attract her. With a last kiss, she set Chloe in a chair. "I'll get you a cookie and a small glass of milk. You stay right here."

Alex sat next to his daughter. "It smells good in here Hannah. What did you cook?"

With her back turned, she said, "Beans and cornbread. I figured we could eat while we visited."

"Thank you. We will enjoy that."

Hannah set the food in front of Chloe and sat on the other side of her. She smoothed the little girl's unruly hair out of her face. "I've missed you, little one, do you know that?"

Chloe took a bite of cookie and chewed, looking at Hannah.

"She missed you, too, Hannah." He paused. "I miss you, Hannah." He reached across the table but didn't attempt to take her hand. "I see your eyes. I know you don't sleep. I don't sleep, either. You mean so much to me, Hannah. You're in my heart."

She closed her eyes. She was in his heart? She'd never been sure of his feelings. Knowing he cared for her this way made it harder to let him go. She met his gaze. "Alex, you're leaving. This, us ... I don't know how to do it. You're in my heart, too. Chloe's in my heart. What will be left of me when you leave?" She bit her lip to stop its trembling. She would not cry.

He scooted his chair back, the shrieking sound grating on her over-wrought nerves. Stepping around Chloe's chair, he knelt beside her. "Hannah, I don't know the answer. I'm trying to figure it out. You're in my head, always, and I think *how can I leave?* I had an idea. What if I ride bulls, and Hannah hires a cowboy to help her? But that is not right. You work too hard,

Hannah. You need a partner to work beside you, to hold the burden with you. Then I think of no more bull riding, and I'm not ready for that."

His eyes were so earnest, when he reached for her hands, she let him take them. She sighed but could think of nothing to say.

He squeezed her fingers. "Hannah, don't give up on Chloe and me."

She sucked in her bottom lip, and now tears filled her eyes. Looking down at their hands, she nodded.

After dinner, they took a ride in the Mule, Chloe sitting on Hannah's lap. It was one of the little girl's favorite things to do. Alex drove all over the home pasture, and they laughed when they went over big bumps, Chloe's preferred choice of terrain.

The sun sat low on the horizon as they drove back in the driveway. Alex set the brake and looked at Hannah. "Thank you for inviting us. My daughter needs her bath. We should go."

Though she knew this was coming, it still hurt. She didn't want to say goodbye to either one of them. "Okay," and she clutched Chloe tighter to her chest.

The little girl gripped Hannah's hair as she stood and walked toward Alex's truck. Her heart grew heavier with each step. The evening without them loomed dark in her thoughts.

Alex opened the back door of his truck and reached for Chloe.

She clung to Hannah's neck. "No. Hama."

Hannah gripped Chloe tight as a wave of intense emotion overwhelmed her. This must be what a mother felt. It had to be. Hannah smiled as tears sprung from her eyes, and she walked a few steps away, cherishing the moment. How long had she waited for this? A lifetime? She needed a moment to absorb it, so that she'd never forget.

Alex stood quietly, waiting.

Chloe mumbled, "Hama," and snuggled closer to Hannah.

Goosebumps skittered down her arms. Every nerve in her body was in tune with the tiny girl in her arms. From somewhere, the song *You are My Sunshine* came to her, and she hummed. Rubbing Chloe's back, she walked several steps up and down the driveway as the little girl gradually grew limp.

Alex stayed still.

When she was sure Chloe slept, she strode over to him. "Thank you for letting me do that."

He leaned in and hugged her, Chloe and all, then gently took his daughter and buckled her in the car seat. Chloe never woke up.

He shut the door with a quiet click and turned to Hannah. "You're good with my *bebê*." Clasping Hannah's shoulders, he eased her into a hug and held her there for a long moment. Kissing her cheek, he whispered, "Don't give up on us, Hannah," and released her.

Chapter Ten

ALEX SAT DOWN AT THE breakfast table the next morning, his eyes puffy from lack of sleep. He couldn't leave Hannah. But riding bulls was his life.

Todd seated himself opposite. "Hey, buddy."

Alex didn't answer right away. Taking a bite of eggs, he chewed slowly, thinking. "Todd?"

"Yeah?"

"You know how much I care for Hannah."

"Yep."

Alex took another bite. "My training is still shit."

Todd looked at him, waiting for him to get to the point.

Alex stopped chewing. "Maybe the doctor is right."

Todd laughed. "What was that I just heard?"

Alex grinned. "I'm serious. My arm is not right, and my pelvis, it kills me when I'm on the weight bench. And driving that damn tractor was torture."

Todd frowned. "That's not good."

"My strength, I don't have it back. I should be stronger now."

Todd stared. "I can see you're planning something. I don't think I'm going to like it."

Alex grinned. "I must know. I have to ride a bull."

Todd slapped the table. "You just said you're not ready."

Alex set his lips in a stubborn line. "I'm ready for a practice bull. I'll know my future when I feel myself on the back of a bull."

Todd blew out a breath. "Dammit, Alex. This is crazy."

He stared at Todd. "I should have been on bulls already." Taking another bite, he said, "I'll call Jody in Dallas. He texted me."

Todd asked, "How long will you be gone?"

"Three days. I want to get back."

Todd nodded. "If you're getting killed, I'm coming to bring your body home."

Alex cracked up. "Thanks."

ALEX HAD CALLED HANNAH Sunday afternoon and asked for some time off. Jody was happy to hear from Alex and, when he told Jody that he hoped to come visit and bring along Todd, Jody heartily agreed. He said he had some nice bulls, so Alex would get quite a work out.

Monday, Todd spent the six-hour drive to Dallas trying to talk some sense into Alex.

He ignored his friend. Bull riders couldn't afford to be scared before they got up on bulls, but they had a very healthy respect for them. Right now, Alex's respect for the bulls he would ride was about as healthy as it could get. He'd never been this busted up and gotten on a bull.

Other people might think he was being stupid. But he had to know if his body could stick on the back of a bull. The pain didn't matter. It would go away when he fully healed. Was his body right, though? Would it ever be right again? He had to answer that for himself.

Jody had a couple hundred acres outside of Plano, Texas. When they arrived, he took them out to the pasture and showed off his latest herd of bulls. "Alex, you sure you're up to this?"

Alex smiled. "That is what I'm here to find out."

Todd grinned. "And I'm here to pick up the pieces."

Jody laughed and gestured to his bulls. "I'm kind of proud of these boys." He stuck his hands in his pockets. "I don't want to see you hurt, Alex. You got busted up pretty bad. I have a kid that will keep the bulls off you this time, though."

Alex nodded. "Sounds great. I'll ride a few. See what happens."

After dinner, Jody lit up his fire pit, and they stayed up late, drinking beer and telling bull stories. The soft firelight flickered across Todd's face. Alex hadn't seen him enjoy himself like this in a long time. He must miss his bull riding days, but he seldom spoke of it. His life was his wife and son now.

Alex closed his eyes and listened to the two men, each talking over the other about tough bull rides. Would this be him someday soon? A weight settled on his chest. Tomorrow he would find out.

Early the next morning, Alex woke with a sense of trepidation. So much depended on today. His very successful bull riding career had come down to the outcome of a few practice rides. He dressed, then headed for the kitchen to find coffee fixings. To his surprise, Jody's wife was already up. "Hey, Susan, do you want me to make coffee?"

She smiled. "I just put it on. So, you're an early riser, too?"

"I didn't sleep good. I don't want to say I'm scared. That is bad luck." He grinned sheepishly. "Man, I'll hurt today. I can say I'm *apreensivo,* um ... apprehensive, yes?"

She laughed. "I believe you can say that without risking bad luck."

Sitting on a bar stool, he massaged his elbow, hoping to loosen it a little before he rode this morning.

Susan sat next to him. "So, you've been staying with Todd since you were injured?"

He'd always liked Susan. She was kind and a good wife to Jody. "Yes, and now my daughter lives with me. Her mother is in Nashville and can't care for her anymore."

"So, you like, have custody of her?"

He frowned. This had been worrying him. "Not really. Debra gave her to me one day and drove away."

Susan drew the corner of her mouth down. "Alex, I don't mean to judge, but that's pretty awful."

Sighing, he said, "My poor Chloe, her life was not so easy. I'll do something about that soon."

Susan got up and poured them each a cup of coffee. "You're a good man, Alex."

Todd walked in, scratching his head. "Hey, Susan. Would you pour me some of that java, please?"

He plopped down on a stool next to Alex. "Don't you sleep, buddy? I heard you tossing and turning all night. You can still call this off. Nobody would think any less of you." He looked hopefully at his friend.

Alex shook his head. "No chance. And, Susan and I agree, I can be apprehensive with no bad luck."

Todd grinned. "Apprehensive? Isn't that a *little* bit like being scared?"

Alex stared solemnly at him, trying not to smile. "Oh, no, it's different."

Todd laughed and slapped him on the back. "Okay, whatever you say, buddy."

Later, as Jody and Todd loaded the bulls in the holding pen, there was no hilarity. Alex faced a series of deadly rides, and nobody liked his chances for success. As promised, the young bull fighter waited in the small arena.

When the first bull skidded to a stop in the alley, Alex looped his bull rope over him and hooked it from underneath, then tied it off loosely. A cowboy let the bull move forward into the bucking area and shut the gate behind him as the other bulls came jogging up the alley.

Alex strode to the bucking chutes and leaned against the bars, shutting out everything around him. Two other cowboys would be getting on the bulls today, so he could catch his breath and pull himself together after each ride. Massaging his arm, he gritted his teeth. Guts and determination were all he had to make it through the upcoming rides. His body sure wouldn't do him any favors. He smacked his fist into his palm. Bull riders rode hurt regularly. He could handle pain. He could *do* this! Bouncing on the balls of his feet, despite how it hurt, he breathed deeply and blew out the air, repeating the process several times.

Todd walked up. "You ready, Alex?"

He nodded. "Oh, yeah."

Jody had a nice set up, and Alex's first bull was loaded in the chute and ready to go. Alex slipped on his glove and climbed up on the wooden rider's platform. His bull was white with some black spots thrown in, and had a single, wicked-looking horn.

Todd stepped across the top of the chute and onto the chute gate.

Jody called, "His name's Wrecking Ball because he lost that horn ramming a wall."

Alex laughed and stepped over the side of the chute, settling his booted foot on the gate opposite. Grabbing the top bars, he stuck his other boot down the side of the bull, and slipped his foot off the bars of the gate, sliding it down as well. Now Alex sat on the bull's back. He could almost hear his pelvis creak. Excruciating agony, too much to be ignored, tortured him. Shifting his weight, he felt for his seat—the particular way his body fit that made him one with the bull. Nothing.

Todd yanked Alex's rope tight.

Alex shifted again, to no avail. He had no more time to waste. Shunting what hurt he could to the back of his mind, he ran his hand up and down the rosin on his rope, creating friction and making his glove sticky. Pulling the tail of the rope tight, he wrapped it around his hand in his own precise way. After pounding it flat with his fist, he was ready.

Now the damn bull had his head between his legs, snorting and pawing the dirt.

Alex slapped his neck hard, several times, and the bull jumped up, shivering.

Todd was long gone by now.

Alex looked at the gate man and nodded.

The gate swung open, and Wrecking Ball flew out of the chute, bucking right out of the gate, and spinning into Alex's arm. In two jumps, Alex was off, flying through the air and landing in a heap. Shattering pain wracked his body. He couldn't catch his breath.

The clown stepped in and distracted the bull. Jody opened the gate, and the animal headed out of the arena.

From the second the gate had opened, everything had gone wrong. The connection he usually felt with his bulls had never been established, and his riding arm? Despite the metal brace, he had no strength in his grip, and his hand popped out of his rope on the second jump. Then there was the pain. Blinding, blazing torture shot up his arm while the agony in his hips each time the bull bucked was, well, if there was a word for it, he didn't know it. This was worse than he'd imagined.

He struggled to his feet.

Todd rushed to his side. "You okay, Alex?" Grabbing Alex's arm, he supported him as he limped to the gate leading behind the chutes.

Alex, through gritted teeth, said, "Yeah. Help me put my rope on my next bull."

Todd sighed and mumbled to himself as the bullfighter handed him Alex's bull rope.

Once on his second, much calmer, bull, Alex searched for his seat again, inching slightly side-to-side as Todd yanked the slack in his rope. Maybe it was the pain from sitting on the bull, but it just didn't feel right. He had never hurt this bad before, and that could be messing with his concentration. Giving up, he secured his hand to the rope, then took a deep breath and nodded to the gate man.

The bull exploded out of the chute, spun away from his hand and slung Alex off his back like a sack of feed. He landed ass-over-hat on the ground. A black wave of unconsciousness nearly took Alex down, but he fought through it.

The bullfighter lured the bull away, and the snorting wall of muscle headed for the open gate.

Alex lay still, taking stock of his hurts. The bull had him out of position with the first jump, pulling him forward. It wasn't just the horrific pain of being on the exploding bull's back. He didn't have his usual strength in his hips and thighs because of his pelvic injury. Nothing was working as it should. But maybe he could try something different. Groaning, he reached for Todd's outstretched hand.

His friend pulled him to his feet. "That's enough, Alex. Come on, don't hurt yourself. It's not worth it."

Alex dusted off his hat and put it back on. "One more." Barely able to walk, he limped to the gate.

With his last bull, he didn't worry about his seat. He concentrated on getting tied on right and would keep completely focused on staying loose and moving with the bull during his ride. Without the strength in his lower body, that was his only alternative. If he could anticipate the bull's moves, he had a chance.

The bull flew out of the chute, whipping right. Alex stayed loose and stayed in control the first buck, and the next. But when the bull changed directions, Alex didn't have the give in his hips to follow it. This time he didn't fall in a heap, but he came close to passing out from the jarring, searing agony when he landed on his feet and fell to his knees.

The bull fighter distracted the bull as Alex pushed himself to his feet. Burning, shooting fire struck his pelvis as he took his first step. He'd failed—his bull riding career was over.

THEY'D PLANNED ON RETURNING to Barbwire the next day, but Alex had no heart for staying longer. He asked Todd if he minded starting the long drive home that afternoon and his friend was all for it. This time Todd drove. Alex hurt too much.

On the way home, Todd tried several times to engage Alex in conversation, but he was in no mood to talk. Coming to terms with the abrupt end to his career overwhelmed him. He had his savings, which was quite substantial, and he could buy his own ranch somewhere. But he'd always thought he would have years to shop around and find a place to settle down.

Dammit, what was he thinking? He'd ridden those three bulls today because of Hannah. Some of the darkness in his mind lifted. He didn't have to figure it all out now. The most important thing was, he knew he wouldn't be leaving Barbwire right away. That changed everything.

Now he had the perfect opportunity to do something about the mess Debra made of Chloe's life. He didn't have a plan yet, but he would make some big changes.

Calmer now, he tipped his hat forward and leaned his head back against the headrest. Closing his eyes, he let his thoughts drift to Hannah. His riding days were over, but if this special woman accepted him, his new life would be even better.

Chapter Eleven

WEDNESDAY AFTERNOON, Hannah stood and dusted off her hands. The wheat had grown well after the recent rains. Her luck might be turning. As she headed back to her truck, her phone rang. Stepping up her pace, she answered before it stopped ringing. "Hello?"

"Hannah, I got back early. Is it okay to come over tonight, about eight o'clock?"

Her heart pounded. Working by herself the last three days had been terribly lonely. What would she do when Alex left for good? "Is something wrong?"

He laughed. "No, Hannah. But this is important."

How she loved his laugh, and how she would miss it. "Of course, please come."

"Thanks. I'll see you."

She could hear the smile in his voice as he hung up. What the heck was going on? Hopefully he would tell her why he'd needed these past days off. By eight, he would have eaten, and Chloe wouldn't be with him. What was so important that it couldn't wait until he came to work in the morning?

She couldn't help it. Her whole body throbbed, anticipating his arrival. He didn't appeal to her just because he was a handsome cowboy. Alex was gentle and kind, tender and loving, and he tried so hard to understand her feelings. She'd never imagined a man could be like him. Despite an occasional language barrier, they were completely in tune with each other.

After feeding at the barn, she headed back to the house to clean up.

By seven thirty, she sat on the couch, drinking her first bourbon of the day and listening to the staccato tapping of her boot. Little tingles kept sweeping up her torso each time she thought of Alex, and, of course, she couldn't keep her mind off him. She was well and truly sunk. He had embedded himself so deeply in her heart, his leaving would devastate her. Tonight, she couldn't regret caring for him.

She stood and paced the room, taking a gulp of Maker's Mark. When had she ever been this reckless with her emotions? Her mother raised her to be a careful child, and she'd stayed that way. But when she was with Alex, she forgot caution. He made her want more for herself, even when she knew she couldn't have more. She was crazy, and she didn't care. At least for tonight.

Headlights shone in the window, and she strode to the door, throwing it open. In the porchlight, Alex's broad shoulders emerged from the truck. She shivered, holding herself back from stepping outside.

He waved and reached back inside, coming out with a vase of flowers. As he came up the sidewalk, she saw that they were yellow roses.

How had he known she loved yellow roses? She smiled, an intense joy rising in her. Alex intuited things about her as no man ever had. She pushed the storm door wide. "They're lovely. Thank you. Come inside."

Grinning, he said, "Yellow will look beautiful with your hair, Hannah. I want to take a picture of you." He stepped past her and walked toward the kitchen.

A picture. Really? She reached up and smoothed her curls, hoping she still looked okay.

"The light is bright here." He positioned her in front of the table and pulled out his phone. "You're beautiful, Hannah. Stand still." Snapping a picture, he moved in closer and snapped another one. "I won't show it to you because you're a woman. You won't like it." He fiddled with his phone for a few seconds. "Ah, both are perfect. Thank you, Hannah. Now I can see you whenever I want."

She felt herself blushing. "Did it really turn out okay?" Having him here, standing close to him, was almost overwhelming. Her body buzzed with desire, and he was just being nice.

"Are you kidding me? Of course, it did."

She groaned and sniffed a rose. "It smells heavenly, Alex. Thank you so much. I can't remember the last time I got flowers."

He quit smiling and looked into her eyes. "You should receive many flowers. I'll change that." He paused. "Can we talk?"

Taking the vase from her, he set them on the table and clasped her hands.

Her pulse raced. He couldn't be leaving. It wasn't time yet. Please, God. Would she get to say goodbye to Chloe?

She must have looked as terrified as she felt because he pulled her into a hug. "Hannah, it's okay. *Meu deus*, you're trembling." He led her into the living room and sat on the couch, pulling her down on his lap. Brushing her hair back from her face, he said, "I have news." Over the next ten minutes, he told her about his experience at Jody's and his decision to end his career.

When he finished, she saw through his brave words to the sadness inside him. Turning his face so she could meet his gaze, she asked, "Are you okay, Alex?"

Gusting out a breath, he said, "I'll miss it, Hannah. I didn't think I would finish bull riding this way." He smiled at her. "I'm also happy. Now I don't need to leave you." Then he frowned. "Unless you want me to go."

Her heart thudded. Joy raced through her veins. He wasn't leaving! She pulled him to her and kissed him hard, proving how much she wanted him.

When she took a breath, he laughed. "Okay, I'll stay." Cuddling her close, he said, "I learned something else while I was away."

He caressed her cheek, smiling into her eyes. "I love you, Hannah. You make me happy."

The love for him she'd been denying for so long swept through her, leaving her breathless. Overwhelmed, voice shaking, she said, "I love you, too, Alex. I always have."

He stood, lifting her into his arms, and strode toward the bedroom. Setting her on the bed, he yanked his shirt out of his Wranglers while toeing off his boots. Laughing, he said, "This time, I'll let you take your clothes off, Hannah."

Her t-shirt over her head, she called, "Already on it."

Fingers trembling in her haste, she stood and dragged her jeans down, forgetting she still had her boots on. Growling, she sat down and kicked them off, then slid her jeans to the floor.

Alex stood before her, naked and, God, was he standing proud.

He caught her looking and pulled her to her feet. "Come here. You forgot something." He quickly slipped her bra off and tossed it on the floor." Kissing her hard, impatiently, he said, "Take off your panties, Hannah. I want to look at you."

As he moved back, she slid them down her thighs and stepped out of them.

His gaze began at her face, lingering and slow, inching its way down her body.

She shivered as if he were touching her and fought to stand still.

At last, he looked into her eyes, cupping her face in his hands. "Hannah, will you marry me? Please, Hannah, will you make me a very happy man?"

She leaned toward him, hot waves of joy flooding her until she couldn't breathe. Her knees wobbled and she placed her hands on his chest to steady her. "Alex." Tears ran down her face. "Yes, I'll marry you. I love you so much."

He picked her up and gently laid her on the bed. As he lay beside her, he said, "Hannah, I'll always take care of you. What Ty did, I will never do. Maybe we will not make babies, but Chloe needs you. I must talk to Debra. Chloe can't live as she did in the past."

Hannah's eyes widened as hope burst alive inside her. Did he mean they might have Chloe? "Your daughter needs a stable life, I agree with you. I know you can manage that for her." She wanted to beg him to take Debra to court, plead for him to do anything it took to make sure Chloe lived with them. But she stayed silent. Alex would do what was right for his daughter.

He leaned down and kissed her so softly she almost didn't feel it. "Hannah, I want to ask you something, but it will hurt when you tell me."

Her heart lurched and started to pound. That could mean anything. She didn't want to hurt right now. Taking a deep breath, she asked, "What?"

He trailed his finger between her breasts and circled her belly button, then met her gaze. "The doctor, he operated on you and then he said you could get pregnant. But you didn't."

Pain stabbed her in the chest. That failure had ruined her marriage. "Yes, he said I had a fairly good chance of getting pregnant after he removed all the cysts, but we tried and tried, and nothing happened. The doctor had no explanation for why I was barren."

Alex kissed her fingers, holding her gaze. "I think your husband was not the right man to make you pregnant. He didn't love you enough." He kissed her again, lingering over her lips. "We will not play doctor, Hannah. If you are pregnant, we will be happy. If you are not, we will be happy, too."

A huge wave of relief flooded her. She couldn't face another marriage filled with trying to get pregnant, or face losing her husband because he got tired of trying and couldn't fulfill her dreams. "I'll be happy with you and Chloe, Alex."

He rolled over and kneed her legs apart. "Enough, Hannah. Tomorrow we talk about our wedding. Tonight, we make love."

She laughed and rose to kiss him, her heart full of joy, and for the first time in years, looking forward to her future.

Chapter Twelve

THE FOLLOWING TUESDAY, Alex held a wire taut as Hannah tightened it around the fence post in front of her. Todd and Becky were ecstatic for them both when he shared his news. The past few days had been a whirlwind of activity. Hannah wanted a small, private wedding, mostly because it had been such a short time since Ty's passing. Though everyone in town knew of his blatant infidelity, she still wanted to keep her ceremony low key.

Todd's son would be the ring bearer, and Chloe, the flower girl. Hannah's friend, Lucy, was coming from Dallas as the Matron of Honor. Todd was his Best Man. Jody and a few of his Brazilian friends were coming down, and, of course, Hannah's parents would attend.

When he could let go of the wire, he tugged on a lock of Hannah's hair. "Have you decided where I'm taking you on our honeymoon yet?" Todd had offered to take care of the ranch for them.

She laughed. "My tastes are pretty simple. Where do you want to go?"

"Oh, no. You pick."

"At least tell me what you like to do, Alex."

"I like the ocean."

She grinned. "Hey, so do I. We could go to Padre Island."

He screwed up his face. "What? Stay here in Texas? You don't want to travel? Anyway, it's cold there now." He wanted to give her an amazing honeymoon. Spoil her rotten.

She threw her head back. "Ugh! Let's go to a warm ocean, then. I'll be happy wherever you are, Alex." Clapping her hands, she said, "So, that's decided. Now, plan away, my love." She pulled him close and planted a kiss on his lips.

He deepened the kiss, wrapping his arms around her and lifting her off her feet. When he leaned back, he said, "I like working for you, Hannah. I can kiss you when I want."

She smiled and narrowed her eyes. "About that. We need to talk finances, at some point. Once we're married, I can't keep paying you wages. We'll be partners."

"Hannah, I have money—"

"Which you worked hard for. Why don't we speak to a financial manager and an attorney, so we can figure out a way to make this work."

He grinned and gave her a quick kiss. "Okay, boss lady. Sounds good." As he bent to pick up his plyers, his stomach growled.

She laughed. "It must be lunch time. Let's take a break."

Nowadays, they went back to the ranch house for lunch, so that's where Hannah headed. As they approached the barn, his eyes widened. Debra's car was parked in front and the woman sat on an upturned bucket in the shade.

Hannah, her voice shaking, said, "Isn't that—"

"Yes."

"Did she call?"

"No."

Hannah clenched the wheel like she wanted to strangle it as she pulled up.

He said, "Let me handle her. I'll go to the house in a little while."

Hannah stared at him, her face pale.

He squeezed her hand. "Be calm, now. Don't worry."

He got out and waited until she drove off before approaching his ex-wife, who now stood, waiting for him. He came to a stop in front of her, hands on his hips. "How are you, Debra?"

Crossing her arms over her ample breasts, she said, "I've been better."

Nodding, he said, "We will talk in my truck."

Once they were settled inside, he asked, "What happened?"

She blushed dark pink and started to cry. "I'm so embarrassed. My big break was a big fat lie. I was a glorified cocktail waitress, and the only singing I got to do was with a karaoke machine while the real band was on break." She sniffed and wiped her eyes with a tissue from her purse. "The place was a dive. One of the girls let me stay on her couch for fifty bucks a week, and it took me all this time to save up gas money to get back here."

What surprised him was she hadn't called him for money. Even if her own phone was out of minutes, she could have borrowed one. "I'm sorry, Debra."

She blew her nose. "Alex, this made me realize I'm fooling myself. I'm not a real singer." She sniffed again and looked down at her fingers. "Just because you want to be, it don't mean you are, you know?"

That gave him an idea. Something that might solve all their problems. "Debra, did you ever want a different job? If you didn't sing, what would you do?"

She stared at him, a faraway look in her eyes. "When I was little, I wanted to be a hair dresser. Then this boy in high school told me I had a great voice, and I forgot all about it."

His pulse climbing, he asked, "Would you still like to dress hair?"

"I think so, but you have to go to school and stuff, and I can't do that."

He reached out and clasped her hand. "Debra, I would like to help you, and I need your help, too."

Her eyes narrowed. " *You* need *my* help?"

He had to convince her. Thinking quickly, he said, "Yes, I do. I'll tell you what I want so you can think about it while I tell you how I can help you. I want custody of Chloe. I can't ride bulls now, so I'll live in one place where Chloe will have a good life."

Debra's jaw dropped. Chloe had been her cash cow for two years.

He must sell Debra on the advantages of giving him custody. "I'll pay for your hair dressing school. Also, while you're in school, I'll give you $1,000 each month. You must work a little, but many people do this. While you're in school, I'll pay for you to come visit Chloe one weekend each month. While you study, you will not need to take care of a small child or pay for her child care, and you will be successful."

Debra looked out her window and was silent for so long he didn't think she would answer him.

He waited. Debra was a good person. This was a huge decision, and he didn't want to threaten her. Nor would he let his daughter leave with his ex-wife. He would give Debra all the time she needed to understand that this was the right thing for her and for Chloe.

At last, she turned to him. "Thanks for not taking me to court, or something like that. I know I haven't been the best mom sometimes. I love Chloe. She'll be happy with you, Alex. I'll take your offer."

He heaved a sigh of relief. "Thank you, Debra." Pulling out his wallet, he handed her $500. "There is one hotel in town. Stay here a few days. I'll have an attorney make papers for us." He squeezed her hand again and opened his door.

A couple of minutes later, as Debra sped down the drive, he thanked God for giving him his little girl.

Chapter Thirteen

HANNAH CLUTCHED HER father's arm and sucked in her tummy, her smile beaming up to the pulpit at her husband-to-be as she strode down the aisle. The front pew on Alex's side was full of tough PBR cowboys. Her two pews were filled with more people than she had anticipated. Her mom asked to invite a few of her life-long friends, and Hannah relented. After all, with her brother's death, this would be the last wedding for her mother.

Alex, looking devilishly handsome, grinned as her father led her up the steps.

The pastor asked in a loud voice, "Who gives this woman's hand in marriage?"

Her father said, "I do," and placed her hand in Alex's calloused palm.

As her father stepped down the steps and returned to her mother's side, the pastor motioned to them. "Please stand before me."

Alex tucked her hand at his elbow and led her to their place in front of the pastor.

The pastor spoke to them about the responsibilities of marriage as her mind wandered to the lavish honeymoon Alex had planned for them on Bora Bora, in French Polynesia. Seriously. Bora Bora. She would have been happy with Padre Island.

As soon as he made reservations, she'd applied for a passport, and it barely came in on time. But she was looking forward to a every second on the exotic island with her new husband.

Fidgeting, Alex covered her hand with his. Her cowboy wasn't very good at standing still.

At last, it was time for their vows. When Todd handed Alex her ring, he held it to her finger and began in his beautiful, deep voice, "Hannah, in your eyes, I have found my home. In your heart, I have found my love. In your soul, I have found my mate." He paused and smiled at her. "With you, I'm whole and alive. You make me laugh. You let me be sad. You're my breath and my heartbeat." Pausing again, he said, "Hannah, *meu amor*, I promise to cherish and respect you, to care for and protect you, to comfort and encourage you, and to stand by your side, forever." He smiled and slid the ring on her finger, gripping her hands as he looked into her eyes.

She couldn't imagine loving this man any more than she did this moment. His wonderful, expressive eyes told her he meant every word of his vows. She wiped her eyes, which had filled with tears, and took his ring from Lucy. Slipping it partway on Alex's finger, she met his gaze, and said, "Alex, you've made me feel more loved than I ever thought possible. I give you all that I am and all that I have. Just as I give you my hand to hold, I give you my heart, my faith, and my life. I choose you today. And I would choose you again tomorrow. I would go on choosing you every day for the rest of our lives. You're my once-in-a-lifetime. I love you, and I'll always carry you in my heart."

Alex leaned toward her and she thought he would kiss her right then.

The pastor said, "In the eyes of God and by the powers vested in me by the State of Texas, I pronounce you man and wife. You may kiss the bride, sir."

She laughed as Alex lifted her off her feet and kissed her soundly. The cowboys clapped and cheered, and the organ played as he led her down the aisle.

Alex's truck, with tattered bull ropes tied to the back and *Just Married* written in white letters on the windows, sat out in front of the little church.

Lucy had provided packets of birdseed for everyone to throw as the couple exited the doors. Alex, who had evidently been warned, grabbed her shoulders, pulling her into a run as tiny seeds rained down on them.

As he yanked open the truck door, she stood on tip toes and whispered in his ear.

He jerked back and stared at her. "*Que?* Hannah?"

With a thousand-watt smile, she nodded.

He lifted her high and spun in circles, yelling, "We're having a *bebê!* We're having a *bebê!*"

She wanted everyone to know before they left town, but Alex had to be first, and it had to be on this, their very own, magical day. Friends and family rushed to their side, yelling and laughing, and patting Alex on the back.

Finally, ignoring everyone around them, Alex had eyes only for her. He leaned down and kissed her tenderly, deeply, lovingly, like the man he was, like the man he would be, forever and ever.

KEEP READING FOR A FREE BOOK.

GET A FREE BOOK!

www.janalynknight.com

ALSO BY JANALYN KNIGHT

DEAR READER

THANK YOU SO MUCH FOR reading my books. Drop by my website at www.janalynknight.com[1] and join my *Wranglers Readers Group* to be the first to get a look at my newest books and to enter my many giveaways. Or, if you like leaving reviews of the books you read, become a member of my *POSSE Review Team* at the Join my POSSE[2] page on my website at www.janalynknight.com[3] and get advance copies of my new books in exchange for leaving honest reviews.

You can also talk to me on Facebook[4] at Facebook.com/janalynknight

Follow me on BookBub by searching for Janalyn Knight in authors and get a New Release Alert when my next book comes out.

Follow me on Twitter with @Janalyn_Knight and be the first to find out when my books are on sale.

Follow me on Instagram at janalynknight where you'll see some of the amazing horses from the refuge where I volunteer

Until next time, may all your dreams be of cowboys!

Janalyn Knight

---

1. http://www.janalynknight.com

2. https://janalynknight.com/join-my-posse/

3. http://www.janalynknight.com

4.   https://www.facebook.com/janalynknight

If you enjoyed Alex's book, please leave a review. Reviews are the life's-blood of an author's living and are very much appreciated!

REVIEW COWBOY FOR A SEASON ON AMAZON

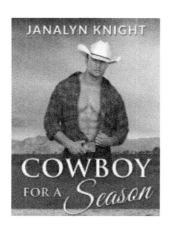

COPYRIGHT

About the Author

Nobody knows sexy Texas cowboys like Janalyn. From an early age, she competed in rodeo, later working on a ten-thousand-acre cattle ranch, and these experiences lend an authenticity to her characters and stories. Janalyn is an avid supporter of the Brighter Days Horse Refuge and totally owns the title of wine drinker extraordinaire. When she's not writing spicy cowboy romances, she's living her dream—sharing her twenty-acres of Texas Hill Country with her daughters and their families.

Read more at https://janalynknight.com/.